Three Dirty Women and the Garden of Death

Julie Wray Herman

This book is a work of fiction. All names, characters, places, and events are the product of the author's imagination. Any resemblance to actual events or persons, living or dead, is entirely coincidental and beyond the intent of either the author or the publisher.

To my parents: Roger Edward and Ann Greer Mills

Thank you for telling me I could do anything,
for making me learn the discipline to try,
and for the love I always know is there.

ACKNOWLEDGMENTS

Thank you to Deb Adams, Dean James, and Megan Bladen-Blinkoff for the unflagging honesty with which you have helped me learn. There exist no better friends. To the Tuesday Night Mystery Writers—Amy Sharp, Kay Finch, Chris Rogers, Amelia Speck, Ann Jennings, Shirl Jensen, and Mary Armeniades—your welcome to a fledgling writer was nirvana. To Randi Faust for telling me I was creative. To Ed Price, Bill May, and Stacey Amos for the cover. To Vikk Simmons for making me face my fear. To Betty Traylor G. for your weekly doses of encouragement. To Sue Mennell and Becky Sallade, the original Dirty Women, for showing me how to bury the body. To Paul for not letting me come to bed. To Edward and Anne for letting me hog the computer. And a huge thank you to Beth Wright, Sherry Lewis, Mr. Blevins, and the rest of the staff at Overmountain for embarking on the Silver Dagger journey. We are so lucky to be working with you.

CHARACTERS

Bascom, J. J.: Pine Grove chief of police; Janey Bascom's husband

Bascom, Janey: partner in Three Dirty Women Landscaping; married to J. J. Bascom, chief of police in Pine Grove

Carrolton, Kaye: county judge

Colter, Nicki: Korine McFaile's friend

Crosley, Mary Faye: a member of the Methodist Church Women

Dominichi, Marlene: dispatcher for the Pine Grove Police Force

Doughty, Jimmy: courthouse handyman

Faulkes, Ruthie Lee: owner/operator of the Cut 'n Curl Beauty Salon

Gerard, Louella: intrepid reporter for the *Cat Springs Inquirer*

Graham, Katie Anne: Susannah Graham's daughter; Dennis McFaile's fiancée

Graham, Susannah: the Merry Widow of Pine Grove; Katie Anne Graham's mother

Harris, Sylvester: political wannabe

Hawkins, Mrs.: townswoman, known for her fine cooking

Hennessey, Kathleen: county clerk

James, Darryl: family practice doctor

Jenkins, Hank: mayor of Pine Grove; married to Sarah Jane

Jenkins, Sarah Jane: town gossip; wife of the mayor of Pine Grove

Manning, Emmie: Frieda's sister

Manning, Frieda: counter worker in the county clerk's office; Sarah Jane Jenkins's best friend

McFaile, Chaz: Korine McFaile's son; family lawyer with a new interest in criminal law

McFaile, Dennis: Korine McFaile's nephew; Katie Anne Graham's fiancé

McFaile, Korine: senior partner in Three Dirty Women Landscaping

Merriweather, Jett: not-so-up-and-coming police officer in Pine Grove

Miller, Claudia: Leon Winters's girlfriend

Osborne, Juanita June: owner of the Green Whistle Cafe

Parker, Reverend: minister, Church of Everlasting Holiness

Patton, Esther: lab tech in the State Crime Lab

Potter, Mrs.: Amilou Whittier's next-door neighbor

Richardson, Reverend Edward: Methodist minister

Smith, Lorraine: Amilou Whittier's former housekeeper

Tucker, Maybelle (deceased): Judge Pierce's secretary; Sally Tucker's mother

Tucker, Sally: Greg Whittier's personal secretary

Whittier, Amilou: partner in Three Dirty Women Landscaping; last surviving member of one of the county's oldest families

Whittier, Greg: soon-to-be-divorced husband of Amilou Whittier

Winters, Leon: up-and-coming police officer in Pine Grove

CHAPTER ONE

"THERE'S A BODY IN THE BED." Amilou Whittier's husky voice emerged an octave lower than normal.

"I told you we shouldn't have had those mint juleps last night," Korine McFaile said to the third woman, who tugged on the wild honeysuckle vine threatening to swamp the lone pine tree before her. The three friends and partners in Three Dirty Women Landscaping, Inc. had toasted the success of their first month in business the night before, and they were all a little worse for wear that morning.

The vine slipped through Janey Bascom's slim brown fingers. It snapped up, butter-yellow blossoms showering Amilou's petite blonde form. Amilou rocked back on her haunches, braced her hands on her knees, and regarded the hole in an ill-placed azalea bed the previous landscapers had insisted on installing.

"I'm not seeing things. It's wearing a ring that looks an awful lot like Greg's wedding band."

Korine and Janey exchanged looks that telegraphed concern. Amilou's husband had run off to California with a gold digger the month before. That was the main reason the three of them were out in the heat gardening instead of sitting on the porch with their tea. Amilou needed the money.

Amilou's marriage had never been a comfortable one. Korine was relieved that she no longer had to pretend to accept Greg Whittier in deference to her friend's feelings. Up till now, Amilou had been pretty philosophical about the whole thing—except for her inheritance, which had disappeared along with Greg. Why she would hallucinate his ring into a flower bed was beyond Korine.

Janey and Korine peered over their friend's shoulder and

— 1 —

shuddered. Amilou wasn't hallucinating. There was a hand; dirt-encrusted, male, and wearing a ring that looked just like dear ol' Greg's gaudy gold-nugget band.

"Dear, sweet heaven." Janey dropped to her knees next to Amilou.

"Do you think Susannah will fire us for finding him on her property?" Amilou asked, sliding her red bandanna off her head and wiping her hands on it.

"One can only hope," Korine muttered, watching Amilou carefully. Amilou was much too calm for someone who'd discovered her husband buried in a former rival's backyard. The scene Susannah Graham had thrown at the church during Greg and Amilou's wedding twelve years before was legendary in Pine Grove.

Korine didn't have to stretch to figure out how upset Susannah would be at finding that Greg was dead and buried in her backyard. All she had to do was to take the sour expression on Susannah's face that morning when she opened the door to discover Three Dirty Women on her doorstep and magnify it.

Susannah had called in some big-city landscaping company the week before to do the area in the backyard that her daughter, Katie Anne, had picked for her garden wedding. Susannah hadn't considered that even the cookie-cutter plantings around the oak tree made the rest of the yard look even worse than usual by comparison.

However, that fact had not been lost on Katie Anne, who wanted every detail perfect for her fairy tale garden wedding. The groom-to-be, Dennis McFaile, had hired his aunt's company, Three Dirty Women, to do Susannah's front yard as a surprise wedding gift for his bride.

Despite her first reaction, once Three Dirty Women was on the job, Susannah had been stricken with an inexplicable fit of garden consciousness, and she asked them to fix what her landscaping company had done. Hence the grisly finding under the new azalea bed.

As Amilou accepted Janey's hand to help her up, Korine caught her first good look at Amilou. Her pupils were unnaturally wide. Her blonde head wove from side to side in denial. With no small measure of relief, Korine recognized that what she'd taken for calm was really numbness, born of shock. Spreading her thumb and pinkie next to her ear, she raised her eyebrow at Janey.

Janey nodded reluctantly and turned away. Korine settled Amilou down on the bench by the side of the curving drive and put her arm around her friend. Amilou's slight form was still, but her hands quivered like small birds nesting on her lap.

Janey pulled her cell phone out of her back pocket and speed-dialed her husband's work number. Being married to the chief of police in Pine Grove sure came in handy when you ran across the odd body or two in the yard.

"Good morning, Marlene. It's Janey. Is J. J. in his office?"

Korine massaged Amilou's tense shoulders and watched her other partner tap her foot waiting for her husband to pick up the phone. They'd been talking about starting this landscaping venture for years, finally acting on their plans when Greg took off. Obviously Three Dirty Women had unearthed much more than they bargained for.

"J. J., sweetheart?" Janey began, using her sweetest honey-do voice.

The annoyed voice of the chief of police floated over the grass to Korine's ears. Janey winced and held the phone out to Korine. J. J. must be cursing again. Korine stood up and walked over to Janey and took the phone.

"Damn, girl, now what've you got yourselves into?" J. J.'s deep voice complained. "And here I was thinkin' that being up to your elbows in fertilizer would keep y'all out of trouble."

"J. J., it's me, Korine."

"Dad blame it, I did it again." The sound of J. J.'s ample behind hitting the polished oak of his desk chair came through loud and clear. "Is she okay—I mean—still speaking to me?"

"What? Oh. Yes, she's still on speaking terms—"

"Good," J. J. cut her off. "I'm sorry to be so rude, Korine, but I asked her not to call me anymore today unless it's an emergency." His voice roughened again. "She knows we've got our hands full—and then some—with those break-ins. Now that they've moved into the city limits, I'm not going to pussy-foot around."

Korine sighed. J. J. Bascom was a good police chief, and Janey a longtime friend, but she really didn't want to run interference for their marriage.

"It *is* an emergency. You know we're over at Susannah Graham's house doing her yard for the wedding? We were working up a misplaced—"

"Get to the point, Korine." J. J. sounded resigned as he interrupted.

She was surprised to find that a mist had gathered in her eyes, making it necessary to dash her hand under both eyes before replying. "It's Greg," she said, looking across the lawn at Amilou.

"Greg? That son of a . . . I heard he was back in town. Has he shown up there trying to get his hands on what little he left Amilou?"

"I wish all he wanted was the rest of Amilou's money. Greg is up to his eyeballs in Susannah's azalea bed. That's why Janey called *you* rather than *Chaz*. We need to report a crime, not engage in a legal battle," Korine snapped. "For heaven's sake, J. J., you married a good woman. Give her credit for brains. Do you remember where Susannah's house is?"

J. J. sighed on the other end of the phone. "Around the corner from Grace Baptist. I'll be right over. Stop touching things. Let me do my job without you girls gettin' in the middle."

Korine flipped Janey's phone shut and turned at the slamming of the kitchen screen door. Susannah came down the walk with a tray of iced tea and her famous lemon bars. She stopped next to the pair standing by the now-open grave. The tea glasses began to rattle on the periwinkle blue tray and then crashed to the ground, pouring their contents into the hole. They were quickly followed by a shower of powdered sugar as Susannah fainted dead away.

J. J. and Doc James arrived a few minutes later to find Korine, Janey, and Amilou leaning over a prostrate Susannah.

"What have you done, Amilou?" Susannah demanded as soon as Doc James roused her.

Amilou's pale face lost what little color it had left. Her deep-set brown eyes turned hard as pebbles as she regarded the softly rounded woman before her.

"What have *I* done?" Amilou's voice rose as she repeated her question. "What have I done? You were the one who insisted that we work here. I wouldn't put it past you, Lil' Miss-Butter-Won't-Melt-In-My-Mouth, to kill him and plant him here just to get back at me. You've never forgiven him for marrying me."

Janey squeezed Amilou's arm in warning. Amilou glared at her partner and shook her off. There was a split second when Korine thought Amilou was going to strike Janey for interfering. Instead, Amilou took a shuddering breath. Her face crumpled as she swung blindly around and walked rapidly over to her battered Volvo station wagon on the drive.

Susannah leaned in a little to J. J. as he helped her to her feet. If she didn't stop it, there might be more violence done—Janey was mild about everything except her husband. Here Susannah's old flame was, dead at her feet, and she still found the energy to flirt. Despite her personal distaste for the woman, Korine felt she needed to intervene.

However much Korine might wish it otherwise, she and Susannah would be related after the wedding. She owed it to her nephew to keep Susannah from making a complete fool of herself. "Would you mind if we took Amilou inside and got her something cool to drink? She's a little overwhelmed by all this."

"Why, certainly," Susannah replied, turning J. J. loose. "I don't know what came over me to say what I did. The poor thing must be feeling horrible. To find him dead after she drove him into the arms of that floozy, Sally Tucker."

Korine felt her face flush, and she took an involuntary step toward Susannah. Susannah took a prudent step backward.

"That's enough!" J. J. barked. "Would you ladies kindly quit dancing all over my crime scene? If you're going to hiss at one another, at least do it inside. I'll be in shortly and talk with all four of you."

The red and white ambulance pulled up the drive behind them as Susannah led the way back to the house. Korine stopped, leaving the back door open a crack. Out beside the grave, J. J. took off his hat and scratched his shiny head. Doc shrugged his shoulders in response to something J. J. said. Korine wondered what Doc said next that made J. J.'s head come up so quickly. Doc shrugged again as the police photographer slung his camera over his shoulder and strolled over to the two men.

J. J. motioned to the laborers he'd brought with him. They worked the flower bed gingerly. Small heaps of dirt grew in the emerald grass next to the bed. They had uncovered an arm when one of the men gave a shout. His dark head bent close over the hole as he leaned in for a closer look. He brushed away dirt with his hand, then held something out to the chief. J. J. spoke sharply and took out his handkerchief to take it from the man's hand. Holding it up to the light, he turned it over. It was a small, white, rectangular envelope.

Korine shut the door. She followed the sound of raised voices into the kitchen. Time to pool their information. While she didn't know what they'd found, she did know who became the first suspect when a husband died. Amilou was going to need their help.

"Did my finding Greg there make up for your losing him all those years ago?" Amilou's eyes were reddened, but dry, as she shook a fist full of tissues at Susannah. The length of Susannah's trestle-top kitchen table separated the women. The chink of ice cubes falling into glasses came from behind the freezer door.

Janey slammed the door and said, "Stop that right now. It won't do any of us any good to say hurtful things. You'll only be sorry later." She put a glass of lemonade down on the table in front of Susannah.

"Don't pull that 'Be Sweet' nonsense with me right now, Janey," Amilou snapped. "It's not appropriate."

Janey looked for a moment as if she would pour the

lemonade over Amilou's head, but settled for setting it carefully down on the table. Korine wished that Janey could let loose sometimes and show her anger, but she kept herself every inch a lady, no matter how difficult her friends made it sometimes.

Korine dropped her hands to Amilou's tense shoulders. "Amilou? Could you use some bourbon in that lemonade to help calm your nerves? I could sure use a little in mine."

Janey turned to Susannah, who gestured toward the cabinet over the sink. Korine took the chair closest to the wall and accepted the slippery glass from Janey. She nodded approvingly as Janey added an inch or so to her own glass before joining them at the table.

"I can't believe Greg had the nerve to come back here," Korine said. "Had you seen him yet?"

"Yes, but why—" Amilou said.

"No!" Susannah blurted at the same time.

The three partners stared at Susannah for a moment.

"No, *I* didn't see him? Or, no, *you* didn't see him?" Amilou asked in dulcet tones.

"Me?" Susannah opened her cornflower blue eyes wide and put her hands under the table.

Amilou stared back at Susannah. Susannah's gaze dropped first. There was no doubt she was hiding something.

Korine covered Amilou's cold left hand with her own and gave it a squeeze. Amilou might be acting as if it didn't hurt anymore, but one look in her shadowed eyes gave the lie to her actions. The pain she'd been hiding from them all this time was etched into the lines surrounding her fine brown eyes. Amilou turned her hand over and squeezed back.

"He came by last night," Amilou said, then paused to draw a shuddering breath. Janey reached out and took Amilou's free hand. Amilou tightened her grip as if her life depended upon the contact with her friends. "He wanted . . ." Her voice broke. "He wanted to come back home."

Janey raised her carefully penciled eyebrow at Korine. Gently, she prompted Amilou, "And?"

"I threw him out," Amilou snapped, bursting into tears.

Susannah's chair scraped over the linoleum as she shoved it back and fled down the hall. Korine and Janey looked at each other. "What in the Sam Hill is going on here?" Korine asked.

"I told you that little witch wanted us in that azalea bed for some unsavory reason of her own," Amilou said through her tears. "It was the only bed in the yard that had already been done, and she told us to start there. Janey, I know you don't like to hear unpleasant things, but finding your husband like that is more hateful than anything I could possibly say about that woman."

At that moment, Korine was feeling quite hateful herself. But not so much toward Susannah. Greg had been a nasty piece of work alive. Dead he might prove to be even worse. "I don't think Susannah knew any more than you did that Greg was dead and buried in her backyard. Even *she* wouldn't be that tacky," Korine pronounced thoughtfully.

"There has to be a logical reason that Greg was buried here at Susannah's," Amilou said stubbornly.

"Susannah had the yard done last week," Janey pointed out. "Very few people knew that Dennis asked us to do it over. Anyone could have come in here and buried him. You know how often Susannah works her yard. Whoever put Greg there took a fairly safe bet that he wouldn't be found anytime in the near future."

Amilou's brows were still drawn down over her eyes. She hadn't been mollified a bit by Janey's reasonable explanation. "Susannah has no plant consciousness. The only reason she sent us out there to redo the backyard was so we'd find Greg's body."

"That is exactly what puts Susannah right out of the picture," Janey pointed out. "Katie Anne is supposed to get married out there tomorrow not twenty feet from that grave. If Susannah knew Greg was buried there, she never would have let us dig him back up."

Amilou's mouth twisted in a wry grimace. "I hate it when you make us be reasonable," she said. "All right, I forgive her. So, if it wasn't Susannah, who was it?"

"Well, it wasn't one of us," Korine said. "Who else knew we'd be here today?"

"Dennis only talked to you a few days ago," Janey answered glumly. "I guess the Harrisons would know since we had to move their yard back to next week."

"They'll have told a few folks." Amilou picked up her drink and took a long sip. "I went in to see Chaz at his office yesterday morning to see what I could do—that was legal—to get my money back from Greg. Chaz said he was looking forward to seeing what we could do with the yard."

"He's my son, Amilou. I told him, so that doesn't mean anything," Korine objected. "That still leaves it pretty much wide open. Who else would want to kill Greg other than you, Amilou?"

"Me?" Amilou turned a stricken face to Korine. "Don't tell me you believe Susannah? I can't hurt a fly, much less my husband."

"Ex-husband-to-be," a deep voice behind them said. J. J. stepped through the doorway from the hall. "Much as I hate to do this, Amilou, I'm going to have to ask you to come with me."

"John Bascom, Junior. You simply cannot arrest one of my best friends," Janey said. "It's not right."

"Neither is this," J. J. replied. He held up a letter, crumpled and smeared with dirt.

Amilou's face stilled, as if the only thing in her vision was the tattered envelope. Then she drew a shuddering breath.

"What is it, Amilou?" Janey gave her husband a warning look. Her café-au-lait skin had flushed, a clear clue that tears weren't far away.

"It must be the only letter I wrote Greg after he left. In which—like an idiot—I told him I'd kill him if he ever darkened my door again."

"I'll call Chaz," Korine said.

"You do that," J. J. said. "Tell him to meet us at my office." He firmly removed Janey's restraining fingers from his arm. "I'm not arresting you, Amilou. I'm taking you in to 'help us with our inquiries.'" His tone was apologetic. "Leon'll be in to see you two and Susannah in a moment." Resolutely, he avoided looking down at his wife's face. Like many strong men, he was reduced to immobility if his wife began to cry. Korine had seen him give in on more than one occasion. She hated it, but this time J. J. was right.

Janey flew out of the back door like hounds were nipping at her heels. For a moment after the door slammed shut behind her, the only sound was that of a horsefly trying to find a way through the screen in the window by the sink.

"Let's go, J. J.," Amilou said.

He turned reluctantly away from the sight of Janey's upright figure standing outside by the high hedge surrounding Susannah's property. Apparently satisfied that Janey would be okay, J. J. turned and gestured toward the front door with his outstretched hand. Without looking at Korine, he turned and followed Amilou out of the room.

Standing up on shaking legs, Korine picked up the phone and dialed her son's private office number. She jumped as the slap of the front screen door hitting the jam sounded its parting shot.

"Chaz, we've got real trouble this time," she said in response to her son's drawled hello. Having passed responsibility into his capable hands, her legs buckled. Korine slid in slow motion down the wall behind her, laid her head upon her knees, and began to cry.

CHAPTER TWO

"ARE YOU ALL RIGHT?"

Korine looked up from her seat on the floor under the phone, knees still clasped to her chest. Above her was the angelic face of Katie Anne, as sweet as her mother was sinful.

Katie Anne's soft blue eyes radiated concern. She held out a well-manicured hand and helped Korine to her feet. "I'm fine, honey," Korine replied. "Just a little overwhelmed."

"Who is it? The policeman out front didn't want to let me in my own house, much less tell me what was going on."

"Amilou's husband, Greg, is dead. We found him buried in your backyard."

Katie Anne's face, which had been looking pinched, turned a queer shade of gray under her light dusting of freckles. "Greg Whittier?" She looked at Korine as if her aunt-in-law-to-be was personally responsible for finding a dead man the day before her wedding. She closed her eyes and pressed her hand to her left temple.

Korine put a hand out and touched Katie Anne's shoulder.

Katie Anne opened her eyes. Her blue gaze was strangely unfocused, as if looking far beyond Korine. "What about the wedding?" she asked.

"Death comes before marriage." At Katie Anne's stricken look, Korine relented. "You'll have to discuss what to do about the wedding with Dennis and Susannah."

"Where is Mother?" Katie Anne asked.

"Upstairs."

"Probably having kittens." The girl's expression was, strangely enough, unsympathetic.

"She took the news pretty hard," Korine equivocated.

"I can imagine." Katie Anne walked over to the sink and filled a glass with water. "I'll take this up and see how she's doing." She hesitated, smoothing her hair back behind her ear. Her hand dropped to her side as she asked, "Where are Miss Amilou and Janey? I hate to leave you, but Mother—"

"Janey's outside, she'll be back in a bit. J. J. took Amilou down to his office to ask her a few questions." Korine wished her voice wasn't so expressive. Showing disapproval of J. J. at this stage was counterproductive.

Katie Anne's blue eyes widened as she stared. Her slim fingers curled around the glass so tightly that the lacquer on her nails showed blood red next to the white of her knuckles. "I knew Miss Amilou and Mother didn't like each other, but I never imagined she'd do anything like this."

"Well, stop imagining it," Korine snapped. "Amilou didn't."

Katie Anne flushed to the roots of her hair. Turning, she fled down the hall. The young girl's rapid footsteps died away upstairs. The murmur of voices told Korine that she had indeed found her mother.

Korine's tennis shoes made no sound on the yellowed linoleum floor as she padded to the back door. She cracked the screen door and watched the slow-motion activity. The bed that they had been working lay open. The new azaleas had been thrown aside every which way, leaves wilting as they lay in the heat of the day. The hole in the center was empty, naked of its contents. She supposed that the ambulance had gone, taking Greg away.

Janey was down on the driveway by the garage, talking to a young uniformed officer that Korine didn't know. As she watched, she heard the unmistakable sound of her nephew's mufflerless Chevy S-10 pull up to the house. As she suspected, not thirty seconds passed before Dennis's tall figure loped around the back corner of the house.

Korine swung the screen door out and called to him. He stood staring at the activity for a moment, then turned and trotted up on the porch. Katie's Anne's fiancé was taller than most, well over six feet. His powerful build complemented Katie Anne's dainty, neat appearance.

"Aunt Korine?" Dennis looked a trifle frantic.

"Katie Anne and her mother are fine. But I'm glad you're here," Korine said, leading the way into the front hallway. "They're in Susannah's room, I think. I'll let Katie Anne know you're here."

"I told you it was none of your business!" The cry, which came from upstairs, seemed to contain equal parts pain and anger.

"The man is dead, Mother," came Katie Anne's low voice. "I can't help you unless you tell me what was going on last night."

The brass umbrella stand next to the front door crashed to the ground. Dennis looked down at his feet, then back up at Korine, as if to ask her who had put those huge things at the end of his legs.

A small grin escaped despite Korine's best efforts not to laugh at the young man's supposed discomfort. He might be big, but he was no slouch at protecting Katie Anne and her privacy, even if it was from his favorite aunt. Korine leaned over and picked up the metal basket. Speaking loudly, she said, "That's all right, Dennis. I'll go up and tell Katie Anne that you're here."

No sooner had she planted her foot on the bottom step, however, than Katie Anne called down, "Dennis, honey? I'll be right down. Miss Korine can show you where the tea is *in the kitchen*, all right?"

Korine about-faced and ushered a silent Dennis into the kitchen. "Tea?" she asked.

"No, thank you," Dennis replied, pulling out a chair. Folding himself into it, he snagged a ripe banana from the fruit bowl in the center of the table. "What's going on out there?"

"Weren't you at Ball High School when Greg Whittier was the coach there?"

Dennis's sandy brown eyes focused on Korine across the table. The oak chair groaned under his weight as he shifted in his seat.

"Coach Whittier? What's happened?" Dennis's hands dropped to the table, his banana forgotten. Korine saw his eyes shift thoughtfully to the hall, obviously thinking about Katie Anne's comment.

"We found him buried in the backyard," Korine answered boldly, watching Dennis for a response. He pressed his eyelids together. When he opened his opaque eyes, they held a familiar appeal.

"Don't look at me like that," she said.

"Aunt Korine?"

She got up and opened the refrigerator to get away from her compulsion to tell her favorite nephew she'd make it all better for him. Dennis wasn't sixteen anymore and the situation was way beyond being fixable. Refilling her tea glass, she replaced the pitcher on the shelf and said, "I wish whoever did this hadn't decided to plant him in the midst of our handiwork. Amilou didn't deserve this. For that matter, neither does Katie Anne."

When Dennis remained silent, she asked, "Did you like him?" Korine filled the Mrs. Teapot with water. Rummaging in the cabinet for some tea bags, she dropped the canister lid on the Formica countertop when Dennis finally spoke, his voice harsh.

"No, I don't suppose I did like him after what he did to Katie Anne."

"Katie Anne?" Korine twisted half around to stare stupidly at him. It was well known what Greg Whittier had done to Katie Anne's mother, but what on earth had he done to Katie Anne?

The young man looked stricken. "Aunt Korine, I shouldn't have said anything. But if anyone would understand, it would be you."

Korine felt off-balance. Ever since she was a small child, people had given her their secrets. They were often uncomfortable gifts.

About a year before her husband, Charlie, had died, the mother of a young girl at Ball High had come to Korine, who was at the time the president of the Methodist Church Women. Greg Whittier had seduced the woman's young daughter, one of the students at Ball High. The family didn't want it publicly known, but they wanted to get him out of the high school so that it wouldn't happen again. Korine and Charlie convinced Greg that he needed to resign. For Amilou's sake, Charlie had found Greg a job at the bank. Korine told Greg that if he didn't stay away from little girls, she'd tell Amilou why he really left his coaching position.

Korine counted backwards in her mind. Katie Anne would have been a sophomore the year Greg moved to the bank. It didn't take much imagination on Korine's part to figure out what Greg had done to Katie Anne. Susannah couldn't possibly know, or she would have been crying out for blood long ago.

Korine stared at her nephew. She'd thought that only Charlie, Greg, and she shared that particular secret. The other family involved had moved out of town several years before.

"How long have you known about Greg?"

"Since you took me in. Chaz told me. Don't tell anyone about Katie Anne, please, Aunt Korine?"

Korine plugged in the teapot and sat back down at the table. Up until that moment, she had never realized that Chaz might have been listening in to her tea-sipping sessions at her kitchen table. She should have known. After all, Chaz often spied upon his dad's poker games.

"I'm sorry Katie Anne had that experience. With Susannah and Greg dating a while back, she must have felt very violated."

"She did." Dennis's jaw clenched.

"Has she been able to put it behind her?"

"Leave her alone, Aunt Korine. Katie Anne had nothing to do with this."

"I never said she did, Dennis. But her mother is a different matter. Susannah might have found out that Greg had bothered Katie Anne. There's no telling what she might have done."

Dennis picked the banana back up and peeled one strip halfway down before replying. "Susannah knows. It hasn't seemed to make any difference to her. Let it go."

Reluctantly, Korine followed Dennis's advice. For the time being. "Well, that still leaves quite a few people who could kill him—metaphorically speaking. How was Greg as a coach?" Korine asked.

"On the field he was fine. Oh, he yelled if you made a mistake, but no more than any other coach did. The problems he had were in the locker room."

Korine didn't say anything, holding her tongue with an effort. Dennis misinterpreted her silence. His face tightened. "I told you Katie Anne never had a thing to do with harming him. She wouldn't have done that."

"Somebody did. And that somebody planted him in Katie Anne's yard. Why do you suppose that is, Dennis?"

Dennis growled, "I can't believe you wound up working right where he was buried. It must have hit Susannah and Katie Anne pretty hard."

Korine pushed her chair back, stood up, and walked over to the counter. The ice from her glass clattered like driving hail as it hit the stainless steel of the kitchen sink. "Or Amilou, who had to find the man she loved buried in the dirt," she reminded him as tartly as she had earlier reprimanded Katie Anne.

He was spared the trouble of apologizing by the arrival of the duo from upstairs. Susannah came into the kitchen looking like a cat that had been dragged backwards through a bush. Katie Anne followed her, looking only marginally better.

Dennis scraped the floor with his chair in his haste to help Katie Anne with her mother. Susannah wilted into the chair as if she lacked bones. Korine suspected it was only her spinal column that was missing. The tea was finished brewing, so she busied herself by heaping spoonful after spoonful of sugar into the hot liquid.

"If only I hadn't let you talk me into hiring your aunt and That Woman, this never would have happened. Whatever shall we do?" Susannah asked Dennis.

What Korine would hardly tolerate from Katie Anne and Dennis was more than she could bear from this sham Scarlet. She opened her mouth and let fly. "You might want to put your energies to better use by thinking about an alternate site for the wedding tomorrow. Or had you realized that J. J.'s yellow crime-scene tape might clash with the bridesmaid dresses?"

Susannah, Katie Anne, and Dennis gaped at her. Susannah and Katie Anne burst into tears. Dennis turned from one to the other, trying to comfort both at once. None of the three seemed to realize that Korine also needed support.

Dennis calmed Susannah, while keeping a gentle arm around Katie Anne. The young woman turned to look up at him. The tension in her face lessened as soon as they made eye contact. The pair turned to encircle Susannah with their arms. Susannah's reddened eyes glared at Korine as she soaked up their empathy.

"Excuse me." Korine let the back door slam behind her as she put distance between herself and the touching trio in the kitchen. Folding her arms across her aching chest, she refused to allow any of the sobs threatening to engulf her to escape. She walked briskly around to the oak tree by the side of the house that was to have played wedding bower the following day.

Putting her hand out, she pressed her palm hard against the rough bark of the tree. After a moment, when she felt back in control of her emotions, Korine lifted her hand and traced the indentations the bark had left in her palm. She knelt down on the soft moss at the base of the tree and ran the tips of her fingers lightly over its fuzzy surface. Closing her eyes, she drew in several deep breaths. The honeysuckle growing on the fence behind her filled her nostrils with its clean fresh scent.

She clasped her blue-jean-clad knees to her chest, forcing herself to dissect the sharp feeling of self-pity. Despite six years' time, it still hurt. When Charlie had died, she discovered that she had many friends. However, friends have their own families—and their own schedules to attend to. After a few weeks of being cosseted and consoled, Korine found herself alone with her grief.

One way she dealt with it was to give houseroom to a certain wild young nephew. Korine had pulled Dennis back from a path that would have kept him far from Katie Anne's door. Dennis's thanks to her was to choose to support his future mother-in-law instead of his own aunt.

On top of that, the young couple's unconscious look of compassion laced with passion had torn the protective covering right off the still-festering wound of Korine's personal loss. How often had she looked up during some silly social function, bored to tears, and met Charlie's gaze across the room to find that same improbable—irresistible—expression on her husband's face?

A shadow fell across Korine's feet and cut off her melancholy thoughts. She put a hand up to shade her eyes and looked up.

Janey dropped to the shady ground next to Korine and sighed. "You're next."

"Any surprises?" Korine asked.

"Oh, yes. But I'd better not say anything until you hear it from Leon. If you don't look surprised when he asks you, he'll slap you into jail along with Amilou." Janey stretched out her legs and leaned back against the tree.

"Are you the same woman who charged out of the house half an hour ago?"

Janey smiled at Korine's raised eyebrows. She changed the subject: "I thought you'd be in with Katie Anne and Dennis helping them salvage the wedding plans."

"Susannah is holding court in the kitchen. I couldn't stand it anymore."

"I'll stay here then," Janey said.

"I do believe you can see the dark side of people, after all."

"You know better than that. I just don't like to dwell on it." Janey stretched, catlike, then wiggled into a more comfortable sitting position.

"Seriously, are you all right?" Korine asked.

Janey nodded, her dark curls falling forward to shield her face from Korine's prying eyes. "I'm fine. Delayed reaction to finding Greg." She nodded toward the policeman who was almost upon them.

Korine took the hands-off warning to heart and let the subject go. Janey had definite walls she didn't want breached. Sometimes friendship was about respecting boundaries as well as building bridges over them. Korine stood up in one fluid movement.

"How do you do that?" Janey asked.

"I'm a practitioner of Hoe-Bo," Korine replied, smiling down at her friend. "Why do you think I got into gardening in the first place? It sure beats exercise."

"Go on, Leon's ready for you." Janey pulled off the scarf she had wound around her neck and used it to discreetly mop some of the glow from her face.

Korine dusted the traces of green moss off her behind. Walking slowly across the lawn, she wondered what the officer said that Janey found so encouraging. A moment later, her jaw dropped as the officer put his question to her.

CHAPTER THREE

"WERE YOU AWARE that Mr. Whittier was living here?"

"I beg your pardon?" Korine's pulse roared in her ears. "*Living* here?" Her voice was a stunned whisper. Had Susannah really thought she could keep that kind of information a secret? In order to stay calm, Korine promised herself that her vegetable garden would get a good workout that evening. You could figuratively bury people like Susannah under the rows so no one knew how wicked your mind truly was.

"Dennis didn't inform you?"

"No." Korine's voice was still faint. Her mind, however, was running like a hamster on speed. So Dennis had known? She imagined "planting" her formerly favorite nephew under the grape tomatoes. Then she remembered the way Greg's hand had looked, reaching up out of the weeds that covered his grave. Suddenly her harmless fantasy seemed sinister. Keeping her eyes trained on the ground in front of her, she said, "I thought Greg was in California with his secretary."

"A business trip?" The officer's voice was even and cool, but Korine wasn't fooled.

Tilting her straw hat back on her sleek graying hair, she met the hazel eyes of the young policeman. "I know you have to ask me lots of questions to tell if I'm a reliable witness. But, if it's all the same to you, let's skip the ones that are outright stupid."

Leon hid what looked like a smile behind his hand and coughed. "How did you get along with the deceased?"

"Not well. Greg left one of my best friends for a silly young thing. I didn't much appreciate that. Although, maybe I should've been glad, because we didn't have to bite our tongues to keep from telling Amilou about all those women."

"And those women would be?"

"Well, evidently, there was still Susannah. I thought that was over long ago," Korine replied tartly. She paused, not sure if she should continue reciting names. She didn't like getting confidences, but she hated giving them away even more. Swallowing, she came to a difficult decision. Murder changes a lot of things. Even when it's murder of someone you don't like. "His secretary, Sally, of course. Marjorie at the bank, Georgette at the Safeway . . ." Korine had ticked off the fingers on one hand and was mentally starting on the other.

"When did these occur?"

"I'm sorry." Her regret was genuine. "I didn't keep track of who and when. I just knew after the fact that he'd been seeing women." Some of those women were no better than they should be, so Korine didn't feel bad about mentioning them by name. Some of them hadn't deserved to be taken in by Greg, and those she felt compelled to protect.

"Can you remember who told you?"

"Not really," Korine lied.

"You've got five fingers on that hand, ma'am. You've only listed four."

"More than one secretary," Korine said, after a quick glance at her betraying fingers. The fifth finger had been Claudia, who had left the bank after the affair ended to work at the Webber insurance office.

Two months before, Claudia had cornered her for half an hour in the church parking lot after a Methodist Women meeting. Korine had managed to listen to the young woman recount the tragic end to her sexual adventures with Amilou's husband without calling her a fool to her face. It wasn't entirely Claudia's fault. Youth was no match for a committed philanderer.

Korine had checked around, finding out about the other women in Greg's life, adding another twenty square feet to her rose garden in the process. She wasn't sure if having affairs with twenty-year-old women constituted breaking his word to her and Charlie.

It had taken a lot of time for her to decide whether to confront Greg about these women—or if she should carry the tales to Amilou. It proved to be harder to inform Amilou of her husband's extracurricular activities than Korine had expected. She was still deciding what to do about it when Greg ran off to California. Finally, Korine was able to refer to him with the loathing she felt he deserved. She just wasn't specific about when she'd begun to feel that way.

"I see," said Leon. "So which secretaries did the deceased have affairs with?"

"The last two," Korine said, distracted by the procession issuing forth from the front of the house. Dennis and Katie Anne supported Susannah between them, Dennis carrying a small Louis Vuitton suitcase.

She looked back at the policeman in time to catch a certain quality of stillness settle around him, as if he were holding himself in check. Belatedly, she remembered that Claudia was dating a policeman. She guessed she knew which one.

"Have you had an opportunity to talk with Mrs. Graham?" Korine asked, deflecting what would surely be embarrassing questions by pointing out the trio.

"No." Leon looked up at her from over his notebook. "Stay here. I'll be right back." He took off at a lope across the lawn, dodging the wilted marigolds by the side of the walkway.

After Leon had swept Susannah and company back into the house, he finished prying more information out of Korine. It hadn't been fun knowing that she'd probably ruined Claudia's relationship with Leon, but she told the truth.

When dismissed, she and Janey opted to leave together. As often happened after a hard day's work, they wound up sitting in the cool of Janey's kitchen, sipping tea and eyeing the remnants of the fudge they'd liberated from the Tupperware container on the counter.

"I wish J. J. would come home so I could ask him what's going on. Do you think he'll charge Amilou?" Janey asked Korine.

"Only if he's listening to Susannah instead of sense. It's

interesting," Korine continued. "She had Greg staying at her house, yet she didn't turn us away this morning when we showed up. Then, when he's found dead in her yard, she denies she knew he was in town. Did she think people wouldn't recognize him when he went out the front door?"

"That *is* odd." Janey picked up the plate and went to rinse it out in the sink.

There was a sharp rap at the back door. Since Janey was elbow deep in suds, Korine got up to answer it. She opened the door to find Dennis shuffling his feet on the back step.

"Oh, come in," Korine said, exasperated that one look from the scamp could dissolve her anger so effectively. She settled back down in her chair at the table. "I suppose you're here to apologize and tell us that Susannah's been clapped in irons and the wedding's off."

Dennis's tone was soft, but reproachful. "Aunt Korine, quit picking on the poor woman. The only thing you know about her is what Miss Amilou told you. How would you like it if someone judged you solely on how you behaved back then?" He pulled out the chair opposite her and swung it around so that he could straddle it and lean on the back.

Janey slid out the other chair and sat down. "Dennis has a point, Korine. It's been . . . what . . . twelve years? We can't let the fact that Amilou is still carrying a grudge color how we look at Susannah."

Korine spread her hands. There were new age spots on the backs of her hands that hadn't been there the year before. Twelve years ago, there hadn't been any age spots at all. Three years before that, she and Charlie had moved back home to Pine Grove. For the first time since high school, they had been forced to weave their extended families into the fabric of their married life. There was one dinner at Charlie's folks' house that she would rather not have to live down. Yet she did, every time she sat down for supper with Mama McFaile.

There was only one problem with Dennis's theory. "How long was he living with Susannah?" Korine asked.

Dennis let out his breath and said, "He's only been—was only," he corrected himself, "staying at Susannah's one day.

He slept in that little apartment over the garage that the Grahams' maid used to use. Susannah only let him stay because he didn't have anyplace else to go."

Korine digested this. She steepled her fingertips together and shrugged, conceding the point.

"When was he last seen?" Janey asked.

"I don't know. Susannah said he went out early last night. This morning, when she didn't see him, she thought Greg was keeping a low profile."

"He was." Unaccountably, it was Janey who said this. "I'm sorry," she said and pressed both hands to her cheeks as they flushed cherry pink. "I can't think what made me say that."

"Well, it's the first tacky thing you've said in front of me since you showed up on my front doorstep looking for work eleven years ago—and I like you more for it." Korine pushed Janey's glass toward her. Janey picked it up and held it to the heat of her face.

"That makes my point though, doesn't it? I'm not the same woman you hired to clean your house."

"We've both come a long way since then." Korine smiled at her friend.

Having regained her customary composure, Janey put the glass down and traced a pattern in the beads of moisture on the outside of the cold glass. "I wonder where he went?"

"That may be the question of the hour." J. J.'s deep tone settled in on the group like molasses, rendering them motionless for a moment. For a big man, he sure did move quietly when he wanted to listen in on a conversation.

"Where's Amilou?"

"Home," he said to his wife's back as she rummaged in the refrigerator.

"And Susannah?" Korine asked. "Did you take her in too? She acted pretty suspicious today, if you ask me."

"Well, I didn't ask you, now did I?" J. J. settled his large frame into the chair at the head of the table. Pulling the nearest glass to his mouth, he drained the water from the melted ice chips in one gulp.

"When should we count on the funeral?" Janey washed

her slim brown hands, then wiped them off on the red-checked dishtowel hanging from the oven handle.

"I think by Monday." J. J. popped the top of the Tupperware container and gave his wife a dirty look when he discovered it empty. She responded by putting a plate of carrot sticks and grapes on the table in front of him.

"But don't you have a lot of investigating to do?" Korine asked. J. J. must think he had everything sewn up if he was going to settle the case that fast.

"Doc James is doing the autopsy right now, and after that we won't need Greg much. Might as well put him back in the ground. Don't need to hold up the funeral to talk to live people."

Janey picked up her purse. "I'm going over to see if Amilou needs anything. She's going to have a lot of people over there shortly."

Korine stood up and put her dishes at the sink. "Chaz was going to take her home when J. J. was done with her. Dennis, you coming along?"

"If you don't mind, I'll stay here for a few minutes."

J. J. eyed him with approval, then said, "You ladies run along now. I'll be gone when you get back. I'll be workin' late."

"I know." Korine could see the love written between the lines of pain on Janey's face as she looked down at her husband. She always worried when J. J. worked. Leaning down, Janey kissed his sun-weathered cheek. She turned to Korine. "We'd better get moving. Amilou shouldn't be alone right now."

The roar of the Cutlass's engine faded into the distance before J. J. began to speak. "I wasn't sure you'd noticed that I wanted to speak to you."

Dennis sat, quietly waiting for J. J. to continue.

"Don't volunteer a lot, do you?"

"No, sir, I don't get myself into as much trouble that way."

"I've hardly seen you since Korine took you in."

"If you'd had to see me, then Aunt Korine would've kicked me six ways to Sunday."

J. J. regarded the young man. Dennis had grown up quite

a bit since he'd first pulled him out of a car, DWI at the precocious age of thirteen. About a month after his Uncle Charlie had died, sixteen-year-old Dennis had been arrested for breaking and entering. Korine had come in to the chief's office, bailed Dennis out, and taken him home with her. She'd saved the boy, plain and simple. But then, it could be a little bit of the other way around. Korine had quickly lost some of that pinched look she'd developed after Charlie died. She had no time to stew when there was a growing boy to look after.

"When did you hire your aunt's company to do that work for Susannah?"

"Last week, as soon as that other company finished."

"Why?"

"Katie Anne didn't want to hurt her mother's feelings, but it didn't look right. I decided that even if Susannah got mad at me, Katie Anne would be happier if Aunt Korine did it over again."

"Janey told me that Susannah was acting kind of surprised when they showed up this morning."

Dennis looked J. J. in the eye and shrugged. "I didn't tell Susannah who I hired. You know how she is about Miss Amilou."

"So Susannah didn't know until today who was actually doing the work?"

"Chief Bascom, when I suggested finishing the yard to Susannah, she about had a cow. This wedding's costing her a mint of money. She like to've killed me when Aunt Korine rang her doorbell. But since I was paying for them, I kinda figured it wouldn't hurt. Katie Anne wanted everything perfect for the wedding, and Miss Amilou has been needing money ever since Coach Whittier cleaned her out. Three Dirty Women seemed like a logical choice to me."

"And you hired them to do the whole shebang? Front, back, sides? Where'd you get that kind of money?"

"I worked two jobs to buy Katie Anne her ring, Chief Bascom. I figured it was worth doing again for a while to give Katie Anne the wedding she wanted. And Aunt Korine said she didn't mind if I paid her over time." The young man paused, fingers drumming a light rhythm on the tabletop. "I've got to admit that I didn't expect Susannah to ask them to work over what the other company had already done."

"So how did they come to be digging just where Greg Whittier was buried?"

"I don't know." The genuine dismay in the boy's voice spoke volumes for how far he'd come since J. J. first encountered him. That thirteen-year-old wouldn't have felt anything for anyone but himself.

J. J. leaned back, the chair precariously perched on the two hind legs. He took a long swallow of ice water and wiped his mouth on the white paper napkin by his plate.

"So, who do you pick for Greg's killer?"

Dennis remained silent. J. J. didn't like the glint he saw in the young man's light brown eyes. He was hiding something.

"Son, don't you mess around trying to figure out who to protect here. I'm having a hard enough time with my wife and her friends in the thick of it. There's no way I'm going to convince them I know what I'm doing. But I don't think we can solve this if everyone decides to go protecting everyone they know. Somebody killed that man, and I aim to find out who."

The front legs of his chair thumped the floor as J. J. leaned forward. "Now start over. And tell me the truth, the whole truth, and nothing but the truth, or so help me, I'll kick you six ways to Sunday and not let your aunt have the opportunity."

Dennis opened his mouth, then shut it again. There was a sheen on his forehead. He cleared his throat. "Coach Whittier showed up at Susannah's Wednesday night asking for a place to stay. She put him in the garage apartment so people couldn't talk. Coach said he'd left Sally and needed a place to get his head back together."

"Were you there this morning when the girls pulled up?"

"Yup." He sounded as if it wasn't his favorite memory.

"And that's when Susannah found out who'd been overhauling her yard?"

"Yup."

"You sure she was surprised? Amilou seemed pretty certain that Susannah knew and hid Greg where he was so that she'd have to find him."

"Believe me, Susannah was surprised to see the ladies. No way she could fake that color."

"I'd've paid good money to see her face," J. J. admitted after a moment of silence.

"She wasn't pleased," Dennis agreed.

"Did you see Greg yesterday while he was at Susannah's?" J. J. pointedly ignored Dennis's bid to defend Susannah.

Dennis looked across the room at the dark gathering outside the back door. He thought a moment, then answered, "Yes, sir, I did. I saw him leave, too. Alive, walking down the street just like you and me."

"The three of them were getting along fine?"

"Yes, sir." Dennis looked down at his shoes.

"You're a lousy liar, son."

The young man's head drooped even farther toward his toes. "Katie Anne didn't want him there. She and Susannah had words about it." Dennis couldn't have looked more miserable.

"Thank you for being frank with me. Don't go thinking that a mother and daughter having words before a wedding is all that unusual. But don't hold things like that back either. You have anything else up your sleeve?"

Dennis shook his head.

"I didn't like Greg Whittier," J. J. said. "Never did. But no son of a bitch is going to murder anyone in my town and get away with it. Now go home, and let me get on with finding out who did this."

"Yes, sir," Dennis said, then fled.

CHAPTER FOUR

WHEN JANEY AND KORINE TURNED in between the tall wrought-iron gates in front of The Pines, they were confronted with the view of half the town's cars parked along the drive.

Amilou's house was the largest in Pine Grove and boasted a driveway and front lawn to match. Still, the driveway was full, so Janey reversed and parked down the street behind Chaz's powder blue Suburban. They collected the cookies and the fruit tray from the backseat and went in to join the sympathizers. Welcoming lights shone from inside. Along the porch, citronella candles burned in their holders.

"If I had a nickel for every time I wanted to plant Hubert—" The slim woman in a startling shade of pink noticed Korine stumble on the first step and broke off.

Nicki Colter, who sometimes filled in as a fourth Dirty Woman, greeted Korine and Janey as they got to the house: "Hello, ladies. Amilou's inside. Holding up pretty well, but still—it's a shock finding your husband that way."

Nicki took their offerings and handed them off to Amilou's former housekeeper, Lorraine, who disappeared with them toward the dining room. They entered the living room to find that Amilou had been cornered by Mrs. Potter, a well-meaning, but always mealymouthed, neighbor. Converging on Amilou, they disentangled the neighbor when Janey cut in and herded the poor woman into the library to help with phone calls to the church ladies.

"Thank you." Amilou's face was pale, but she showed no sign of wanting to run away into the night, which Korine suspected she would do under the same circumstances.

"Why don't you sit down and try to relax."

Amilou raised an incredulous eyebrow at her. "I can sit,

but don't expect miracles."

Korine linked her arm through Amilou's and dragged her outside. They settled in the wicker furniture around the corner of the porch by the bedroom. The evening serenade was in full swing. The high-pitched sounds from the bats scooping up insects and the faint hum of traffic from the street formed an unusual, soothing composition. It was punctuated occasionally by the slam of car doors as people came and went.

"You know what?" Amilou's voice sounded tired. "I've been wondering all day what happened to the girl Greg ran off with. She might have been a faster learner than I am and left him right off the bat. Which would explain why he wanted to come home. Or, she might have killed him because he'd left her to come home to me."

Korine sat silently, thinking unkind thoughts about Sally Tucker. Amilou was much smarter than Sally, so Korine didn't think that Sally would have figured Greg out yet. At least she wouldn't have if the money were still holding out.

"I never trusted Sally," Amilou said, fingering her feathered blonde hair. "Too much like her mother for my taste. Always neat as a pin. She always wore white, even after Labor Day, because she felt it set off her bouncy, shiny, blue-black tresses."

"That's right, I forgot that Mrs. Tucker worked for your daddy." Korine sat straight up in her chair. "Could Sally have been buried with Greg?"

Amilou stared at Korine. "No way Sally was in there with Greg, or J. J. would still have me down at the jail."

"That young officer, Leon, asked all kinds of questions. Mostly about you, but some about Sally, too." Korine shook her head to clear it. "You're right. Now that I think about it, he sounded more like they didn't know where Sally was."

"What did they ask about me?" Amilou's eyes narrowed. "Never mind, I probably don't want to know. I do wonder if they've found that Sally-girl yet. I can't wait to hear what she has to say for herself."

"I second your vote for her as the guilty party. She had

more reason to kill him than you do. You'd already gotten him out of your life."

"Do you mind if I join you?" Janey sat down in the third chair.

"Not if you share those." Korine indicated the plate of sandwiches that Janey had set on the footstool in front of Amilou. Amilou and Korine helped themselves, then all three settled back in the chairs.

"J. J.'s going to be so disappointed that he missed Mrs. Hawkins's funeral casserole," Janey said.

"After the way he grilled me today, I don't feel a bit sorry for him," Amilou retorted. "I wouldn't let him in the door."

Korine shot Amilou a warning glance, while Janey pursed her lips, then raised her sandwich to take a bite.

"I guess I should apologize for that." Amilou pressed one hand to her flushed cheeks. "I didn't mean it that way."

"I know," Janey said, her voice distant. "No one ever does."

"I'm going in to freshen up my drink. Can I get anyone else anything while I'm there?" Korine asked.

Receiving a duet of acceptance, Korine picked up the glasses and went back inside. The first person she saw as she came through the door was Sarah Jane Jenkins, the mayor's wife.

Sarah Jane made a beeline for Korine, running her to ground next to the lemonade pitcher in the dining room. "How is she doing?"

"As well as can be expected, Sarah Jane."

"Where is Amilou? She ought to be out here receiving her guests."

"This isn't a party," Korine fired back tartly. "She's having a hard time right now."

"That's right. I guess after spending half the day being cooped up in the police station, she deserves a little rest. All this excitement. And after she was up all night, too."

"Excuse me?"

"She was out late last night."

"That's right," Korine answered absently. "She came over to discuss some preliminary plans with Janey and me." After discussing those plans, Korine had mixed up a batch of mint juleps for a celebratory toast to the success of their first month in business as Three Dirty Women Landscaping, Inc.

"Work, work, work. I don't know how y'all do it. Deliveries at midnight; dead men in the morning." The frantic waving of an ill-dressed, and completely unfamiliar, woman in the corner captured Sarah Jane's attention, but not before she took satisfied note of the stunned look on Korine's face.

Korine made her escape as Sarah Jane crossed the room. Silently, she blessed the gesticulating stranger for distracting Sarah Jane before she could drop any other bombs on her.

Amilou had been late for the impromptu celebration, coming in a little after nine, and she had left early, after the toast, pleading a headache. Korine had put it down to the fact that Three Dirty Women had been getting almost too busy in such a short time. Now she wasn't sure. Where would Amilou have been going at midnight?

J. J. pulled his cruiser over to the curb behind the small, battered white Chevy pickup parked in front of Susannah Graham's house. There was no getting around it, her yard looked pretty bad. Dennis was right to have hired the girls. Around back, where crime-scene tape surrounded the gaping hole in the bed, it looked even worse. Janey had told him earlier that Dennis had mentioned postponing the wedding until after the funeral. If they still wanted to get married at Susannah's, that would be a good idea.

Grabbing his cell phone from the seat next to him, he dialed the office. No answer. He was going to have to speak to Marlene about the number of bathroom breaks she took. Cutting the ring short with a touch of his thumb, he undid the top button on his uniform and ran a bandanna under the collar of his shirt. It was more than time for the temperature to cool down. He stepped out of the car, welcoming the evening breeze that floated over the well-tended lawns. Slamming the door, he walked through the gate in the hedge and began to make his way up the front walk.

He stopped, giving himself a minute to mentally compose

a few questions for Susannah and her daughter. Glancing back at his car, J. J. wished that Marlene had answered his call. If they were going to pay her overtime during this murder investigation, the least she could do would be to man the damn phone.

He tugged a packet of Marlboros from his pocket. With the smooth motion of long practice, he cupped his hand around the tip, lit the cigarette, and then shook the match out while exhaling.

Amilou Whittier was no fool. J. J. didn't think she would bury her husband in a flower bed when she would just go digging him up again the next day. But then again, perhaps she was a very smart woman. Digging him up in front of witnesses would explain away any evidence they found of her presence in the bed.

Bringing the cigarette to his mouth once again, J. J. focused in on something at the edge of the house. A slow frown creased his face. He went back to the car for his camera, then went to check it out.

Ten minutes later, J. J. slammed the trunk of his car on the evidence bag he had carefully placed inside. He turned and rested his backside on the trunk. Surveying the neighbors' houses, he wondered what had possessed Susannah to let her property go like she had. That hedge along the front obscured her whole property.

It had made for a very frustrating time of it when Leon talked with the neighbors to see what they'd noticed the previous evening. J. J. wished Susannah had knocked down those bushes before whoever it was had buried Greg. It would make their job a whole lot easier if somebody had been able to see what had happened the night before.

One of the first questions he intended to ask Susannah was why she'd had Dirty Women redoing work she'd already paid for. Since Susannah was obviously not a yard person, J. J. had to wonder if it had been dumb luck that had led to their discovery.

There were more than three women who might have wanted to kill Greg Whittier. But what he'd heard from

Amilou and Janey about the events of this last week focused attention on Sally, Susannah, and Amilou. With a little more evidence, he'd be able to concentrate his investigation on one of them. J. J. unfolded his arms and set out up the walk again. This time he made it to the front door. He pressed the bell and stepped back to wait.

Susannah peered around the door as if she expected to see a ghost. J. J. could practically see her pull her flirtatious manner out of her pocket and plaster it across her face. She had made every effort to snare a man—any man—since her husband died fifteen years ago. So far, no one had taken her up on more than a pleasant evening. And here she was, trying it out on happily married J. J. himself. It was really kind of pitiful.

"Ma'am. May I come in?"

"Why, certainly. Let's go in the living room. Much more comfortable for a big man like you."

J. J. scowled at the woman's back as he followed her into the living room. True, he'd rather settle into the deep club chairs than those creaky little chairs she kept in the kitchen, but he disliked his weight being a consideration.

"Can I get you something to drink?"

"No, thank you." J. J. leaned back into the softness of the chair. "Leon told me that you were too distraught earlier to speak with him. I'll need to get your statement now." Try as he might, he couldn't keep a note of displeasure out of his voice.

Susannah leaned forward, showing some fine-looking cleavage in the process. "I was upset, Chief. That woman has ruined my life before, but it's going too far to have her ruin Katie Anne's wedding day."

"That woman?"

"Amilou My-Family-Is-Holier-Than-Yours Whittier." It was interesting how hate could transform those soft, flirtatious features into something altogether different. J. J. crossed one leg over the other and pulled up on the toe of his shoe to settle it firmly on his knee. He cocked one eyebrow at her and waited.

His patience was wasted. Katie Anne poked her head in the doorway. "Sorry, I didn't realize you were here," she said when she saw J. J.

"We'll be through here shortly," he said.

"Go on, dear. I just have to tell Chief Bascom all I know about this mess."

Katie Anne retreated to the kitchen, where a low murmur of voices confirmed his earlier assumption that the bride had company.

J. J. waited. Despite her statement to her daughter, Susannah was having trouble getting started with the telling part.

Finally, she shrugged her shoulders and raised her hands in defeat. "Look, I don't know how she got him there. I just know she did."

"I understand that you and Amilou were rivals for Greg's attention a while back. How does that translate into Amilou's wanting to ruin Katie Anne's wedding day?"

"I think that was icing on the cake for her. Greg and I drifted apart before he got involved with Amilou. But she's never forgiven me for my special friendship with Greg."

J. J. had heard that it was the other way around, but he didn't interrupt her now that she'd started.

"I'm not saying that Amilou killed him because of that," Susannah went on, "although she's meaner than molasses when she's crossed. When we were three, she got mad at me for winning at jacks. She pushed me clean off her front steps. Amilou had more than enough reason to do away with Greg, between Sally and the loss of all that money."

J. J. decided to let her continue. So far, she hadn't come up with anything new. However, if the woman kept going, something useful was bound to fall out. "Where do you think she killed him?"

"At her house, of course."

"Amilou's a small woman. How do you think she got him all the way over here? And why would she bury him here?"

"She's stronger than she looks. All that grubbing in the dirt gives a woman muscles. As for why she buried him here, it was jealousy, pure and simple. He came to *me* when he left that other woman, not Amilou."

"Why *did* he come here?"

"He never did say. But"—Susannah leaned closer and whispered—"the minute I saw him standing in the doorway, I thought that he was frightened."

"Frightened of what?"

"I don't know. But he wouldn't talk about either Sally or Amilou at all, just kind of pressed his lips together and shook his head at me."

"You put him up in the garage apartment?"

"Yes. People talk so, but I couldn't turn him away. After all, he was an old friend."

"How long have you known Greg Whittier?"

"Since high school. We weren't close, you understand, not then. He and I both attended Davidson. That's where I met my husband. After Hal died, Greg called to express his condolences. Soon after, we started seeing each other. For a while I thought he might be something special." The fine lines surrounding Susannah's mouth tightened, then she treated J. J. to another honey-sweet smile.

He rewarded her with a specialty look of his own. It was the I-know-what-you're-not-telling-me look. It'd gotten Bailey Longfellow to fess up to robbing Klein's Hardware the week before, but it didn't work on Susannah.

Since he didn't think dragging her down to the station would make her be any more forthcoming, he changed tactics. "How did Katie Anne get along with Greg?"

"Katie Anne?" Susannah flushed, then opened her blue eyes wide. "Why, she loved Greg. I did hope that he would be a father to her after Hal died. But it wasn't meant to be."

J. J. looked at her through bushy eyebrows. Her flush deepened, but it seemed to be more a matter of habit than embarrassment.

"It was a cruel twist of fate that led you to suggest Amilou start over in that bed this morning," J. J. said.

"Well, if you say so. Personally I think she started there so she could find him first off and not have to finish the job."

Susannah's anger was patently real.

J. J. thought a minute, then decided he would have to ask the question. "Susannah, did his fondness for young girls have anything to do with your decision not to marry Greg?"

Susannah rose and walked to the fireplace. Slowly, her finger traced the creamy paint on the front of the mantel. "I'm not going to pretend I don't know what you're asking."

She turned around and faced him. For once, there was no vestige of coquetry in her manner. "It would take a special woman to keep Greg Whittier satisfied enough that he wouldn't stray. And he did have a fondness for young women. But I can tell you true, Greg would not have touched my daughter. Not now, not ever."

For once, J. J. was willing to swear that she believed what she was saying. However, if his personal assessment of Greg was anything to go by, it wouldn't have bothered Greg a bit that this particular pretty young woman was the daughter of an old flame.

"So they had no contact after you stopped seeing him?"

"No. None."

"Dennis played ball for him."

"That's true. But Katie Anne and Dennis were high school sweethearts; she didn't play on the team." Susannah bit her lip. "No, Chief, I'm afraid you'll have to take a good look at Miss Amilou if you want to find someone with vengeance on her mind."

"Mom?" Katie's Anne's voice called from the back of the house. "There's a phone call for Chief Bascom."

"You'd better take it here." Susannah indicated the phone in the hall.

"Bascom," he answered.

Listening intently, what J. J. heard on the other end made him swear. Susannah backed away a step. "Sorry," he said automatically. Janey didn't seem to be able to get him to stop cussing, but he supposed apologizing for his language was a step in the right direction.

J. J. slammed down the receiver. "I've got to go." He would have liked to talk to Katie Anne before Susannah warned her off. But perhaps it was better this way. They could stew a while, then he'd swing back by the next day.

He rushed back down Susannah's front walk, hitching his trousers back up around his waist as he went. Hopefully, in the morning, he'd be able to get something useful out of Susannah. That was, if she knew anything useful. J. J. turned the key in the ignition. He swore under his breath again as he picked up his cell phone to call and leave a message for Janey. He headed out thinking that there was entirely too much crime in this sleepy town.

CHAPTER FIVE

"LEON, WHY'N SAM HILL can't criminals take a day off?" J. J. looked at the scratches on the lock of the back door of the old train depot. Inside, flashes of light showed the police photographer at work. J. J.'s stomach growled. He hadn't had time for lunch, and while he'd hoped to get some dinner, he hadn't gotten there yet.

"Sir?" Leon took one look at J. J.'s face and thought better of what he'd been going to say. He led J. J. through the doorway and down the hall to the now-pseudo-rustic lobby of the Pine Grove Depot Bed & Breakfast. When the train canceled its stop at Pine Grove thirty-some years before, the old depot had fallen into disrepair. It had been salvaged by out-of-towners who thought it'd make a cute little restaurant. Trouble was, Juanita June's cafe was popular, and Pine Grove was smallish for two places. The Depot had never attracted enough customers to make a go of it.

The owners had given up, sold the place to somebody else, and gone back north. The new folks had decided to refurbish the top floor and convert it from a failed cafe into a Bed and Breakfast. J. J. hadn't thought this incarnation would go over any better than the cafe had, but he'd heard that the new manager was pleased by the number of people who came up from the coast trying to escape the summer heat.

There had been a rash of burglaries in the summer cabins in the hills around town. J. J. was pretty sure vagrants were responsible, but so far no one had seen anything. Up until that point in time, they'd all been in uninhabited buildings. This was different. A small group of people sat around a large circular table in one corner, and his new uniformed officer, Jett Merriweather, was taking names.

"Anybody hurt?" J. J. asked Leon.

"No, but the manager's room is a wreck. If you'll come with me, I thought you'd like to take a look at that."

Following Leon up the steps, J. J. wondered who in his right mind would pay upwards of a hundred dollars a night to stay in a rustic place like this. There wasn't enough lighting in the hallway to find your way to the door, let alone see what you were paying for.

They turned right at the top of the stairs and walked through the first door on the left. Everything in the room had been dumped on the floor. There was a considerable lot of stuff. The mattress from the queen-sized pineapple-post bed lay slashed open on the floor. Drawers from the cherry chest against the wall had been emptied of their contents, then flung onto the bed. The contents themselves were ripped and shredded. Scraps of white material littered the floor like snow. Not a stitch could be recognized for what it had been. One thing J. J. knew, it didn't look a thing like the previous B&E's they'd had.

"Who's the manager?" J. J. asked.

"Sally Tucker," Leon answered. "She started this past week."

J. J. closed his eyes and massaged the back of his neck. "Please tell me she's not under all this stuff."

Leon drew himself up reproachfully. "I would have mentioned that right away. The maid said Miss Tucker was out late last night, came in about six this morning, barely in time to get breakfast for the guests. About five minutes after she finally made it up to her room, she left—in a hurry, according to one guest.

"When the cleaning girl got done with the rooms this afternoon, she came up to tell Sally she was leaving. She didn't get an answer when she knocked, so she went on in to drop off the fresh towels."

"She's just now getting to the phone?" J. J. growled.

"She was scared. The girl left the door unlocked, thinking that someone would need Sally, try the door, then find the room in this condition and call us for her."

"So why'd she finally call?"

"Heard the news about Greg's death."

"I see," J. J. said making a note of the girl's name and address in his notebook. "No idea yet where Sally might have gone?"

"No, sir, not yet. But we'll find her. How many places could she be?"

J. J. looked at his officer. With some effort he managed to keep his voice level. "I'll count on hearing from you pretty quick then."

Leon paled.

"Get pictures of Amilou Whittier and Susannah Graham, and show them to the guests. Ask if any of them have seen either of these ladies around here in the last day or so." As he turned to leave Leon to his search, J. J. added, "And check the room for Greg's blood type."

Leon's Adam's apple bobbed once as he swallowed. "Yes, sir."

"I'll talk with you later. Get me a report."

"Yes, sir," Leon said to the chief's back as he strode out of the room.

The trouble with all this, J. J. thought as he drove along Elm Street, was that he wasn't sure which suspect to talk to first. On the surface of it, it might be a B&E gone wrong. But given the identity of the room's occupant, and the sheer malice involved in the destruction of the clothing, he was pretty sure he knew who had done it. Janey was not going to be happy. He picked up the phone.

"Marlene?"

"Yo." Their dispatcher had moved down a few years ago from New Jersey, and try as he might, J. J. couldn't break Marlene of some of her bad habits.

"You been in that ladies' room again?"

"Is that a personal question, Chief?"

J. J. backed down, as he always did. "Do you happen to know who-all bought the Depot from those folks?"

"No, I don't. But Juanita June would know. She knows everything. Except that Sally Tucker was pregnant."

"What?" J. J.'s car swerved toward the curb. "How do you know that?"

"Doc James stopped by with Greg's autopsy report. He mentioned how sorry he was for Sally, what with the baby coming and all, now that Greg was dead."

"Well, I'm glad he told you, but it's unlike him to break confidence with a patient."

"Just a slip of the tongue. We've gotten to be good friends. By the way, he's going to visit his brother in Jesus Creek."

"Doc's leaving town? Now?"

"Doc left his number over there. Besides, he'll be back in a day or so. Said he needed to get some fishing in to clear his head."

"Sally pregnant." J. J. thought for a moment and came to a decision. "I'm going over to the Green Whistle and get myself some supper and see what else Juanita June might know that could help me. Then I'm heading over to The Pines. Chaz was taking Amilou home. With the way things are going today, Janey will be there too. I'll have a grand ol' time."

J. J. cut off the call. He pulled out into the intersection and gunned the motor.

Pulling into the lot outside the Green Whistle, J. J. counted the cars of ten of Pine Grove's leading citizens parked there. Must be a town meeting he wasn't aware of. He slammed the car door and went on inside.

When the Depot Cafe had opened, Juanita June decided she needed to convince the population that the Green Whistle was as up-to-date as any new place. Trouble was, her idea of sprucing up consisted of changing the name from the Blue Whistle and painting the whole place an apple green. It made J. J. a little bit bilious, but she'd meant well.

"Coffee?" Juanita June stopped by the booth as soon as J. J. slid in.

"Yes, please." He turned the cup right-side up for her. She poured a stream of thick black gold in. Sipping at the hot liquid, J. J. felt a rush of energy fill him. "What's going on over there?" he asked, pointing with his mug toward the group huddled in the corner.

"Sylvester Harris's thinking up strategy for his next election bid."

"He's lost three times running. Those men have never supported him before. What makes him think they'll be on his side this time?"

"Oh, he's not running for mayor this time. He's running for Sheriff." With a grin and a wink, Juanita June went to pour coffee for a new arrival. She took the order, turned it in to the cook, and then returned.

"What's your pleasure?"

"I'll have the chef salad."

Juanita June stared at him. Sticking her pencil behind her ear, she laid her hand on his forehead. "Nope. Not sick. What's gotten into you?"

"Too much of your good cooking. Janey's got me on a diet."

Juanita June said, "Man can't live on collard greens alone."

J. J. felt his face go red. With an effort, he held his temper down. Janey was lighter than many of the tanned women playing tennis out at the club. He'd gotten a lot of grief when they first started seeing each other. Some folks felt that since some of her ancestors had come over from Africa on a slave ship, Janey needed to be more humble than to marry a white man. He'd ignored them because those same people hadn't seen too much out of the ordinary when her first husband, also white, beat her regularly. He'd thought of Juanita June as a friend. It had never occurred to him that she might look at things differently.

J. J. studied her. In the interest of getting answers to the questions he came in for in the first place, he swallowed what he really wanted to say. "Long day?" was what finally came out.

Juanita June shifted her weight to the other foot under J. J.'s eye. "I didn't mean it that way. Too much listening in over in the corner there." She gave a meaningful nod with her head.

"What?"

"I'm just cluing you in to an election issue." For a side step from a tacky comment, it wasn't bad.

"Sylvester can't beat that dead horse. He can run for Sheriff all he likes. I'm hired by the City Council, and no cow-faced ignoramus is going to set me off . . ." J. J. stopped and studied the menu closely. "Ahem. I'll have the country-fried steak and a baked potato."

Juanita June retrieved the pencil and wrote the order down. "Coming right up."

Hank Jenkins, Sylvester's political nemesis of the last two out of three elections, strolled in. His stride slowed when he saw the group in the corner. Slowly, Hank's head panned, taking a survey of the other occupants in the place. A smile broke out on his face when he spotted his old friend sitting alone.

He slid into the booth opposite J. J. "Wrapped things up yet on the murder this afternoon?"

"Nope." J. J. sipped his coffee, studying the men in the corner. Every now and again, one of them would turn around in his seat and stare back at him. No smiles or greetings were exchanged. "Happen to know what's going on over there?"

Hank shook his head. "Tell me the worst. What is that bunch of troublemakers up to now?"

"I would guess that means no."

"Is there any way to arrest them?"

"Not until you pass a law against being stupid. From what Juanita June said, Sylvester's going to run for Sheriff this time, on account of because he doesn't realize that I'm appointed by City Council and not by the Sheriff."

"That Sylvester's a one-man circus. Coffee and a BLT, Juanita June."

Juanita June just looked at Hank and rolled her eyes. "And has your wife got *you* on a diet too?"

"Honey, I'm only saving room for your cobbler." Hank picked up the coffee cup Juanita June had filled, raising it in a toast. "I eat light during berry season just so I can come here."

"That old Depot Cafe never had blackberry cobbler," J. J. began, "only some flat things wrapped around peaches. Not as good as yours. I'll bet you were relieved when they went out of business."

"You know, they weren't bad folks. A little fancy, and from up north of course, but still pretty nice. I was sort of sorry to see them go."

"So when the new owners opened up, you went over to welcome them to town?"

Juanita June looked down at J. J. "It took you long enough to ask. The new owners are Sally Mae Tucker and her beau, Greg Whittier, whose wife, Amilou, found him dead this morning. I do love to see men at work. Marlene called me." She trotted off to fill more coffee mugs.

"Told you, didn't she?" Hank asked rhetorically.

"Mmm." J. J. stared after Juanita June's retreating back. "I have one or two secrets up my sleeve. I'll still stay for supper. She didn't tell me everything I need to know." He propped both elbows on the table. "Hank, I've been meaning to ask you something. Does it ever bother you about Janey and me?"

"J. J., I'm so happy you finally found somebody who can hold onto you for more than a New York minute, that I couldn't care less if she was from Mars. That *is* what you're asking, isn't it?"

"Mars?" was all J. J. could think to say.

Sylvester stood and wound his way to the men's room. Both Hank and J. J. watched his progress. "I wish I could arrest Sylvester for this murder and make everybody happy."

"Me, too," Hank said, with heartfelt honesty. "Bring me up to date. You know who did it yet?"

"Maybe, maybe not." J. J. never told Hank anything about cases while they were open, but that didn't stop Hank from asking. "You happen to know when those two got back in town?"

"Frieda told the wife that Sally was in her office looking stuff up last Wednesday. Said it'd rock the town when we all found out." The county clerk's secretary lived next door to Hank and was his wife's best friend.

"What are you talking about?"

"I'm just telling you what Sarah Jane said. Evidently, Frieda told her that Kathleen Hennessey—the new county clerk," Hank added at the look of confusion on J. J.'s face, "—anyhow, Kathleen said this would blow the top off a lot of things. Before you get all excited about talking to Frieda, Sarah Jane said that she went to her mother's in Charlotte this weekend. If you like, I can call her and ask her to give you a call."

"Actually, I'll probably go ahead and call Kathleen at home."

"You just don't want Frieda telling Sarah Jane."

J. J. stared into space. "Did you know Juanita June missed a spot up there by the ceiling. I'd forgotten this place used to be Robin's Egg Blue."

"I left it that way on purpose so I would know what color to order when I decided I was tired of Apple Green." Juanita June put their plates down in front of them.

"When did Sally and Greg come back to town?" J. J. asked, opening his napkin. "And why were they living separately, if they were going to run that B&B together?"

"Thank you, Juanita June, for a wonderful looking meal," Juanita June said through gritted teeth. "If you really want to know, I heard Sally threw him out Wednesday night." She stalked away. "Men."

J. J. and Hank looked at each other. J. J. raised a hand in defeat. "She told me to ask her if I had a question and not to pussyfoot around, so I did. Now, she stalks away muttering, 'Men.'"

Hank shrugged. "Don't fight it. But I sure am glad she got mad *after* our plates were here and not before." Next to their dinners were two bowls of steaming hot blackberry cobbler. Since the cobbler was topped with rapidly melting vanilla ice cream, they ate dessert first.

CHAPTER SIX

AFTER HEARING WHAT SARAH JANE had to say earlier about shirking her duty, Amilou had gone inside to greet people. She had escaped back outside a scant half hour later, pleading a headache after making the rounds through the crowded rooms. Korine had followed her, head pounding in sympathy.

After a few moments of talking about nothing, Korine girded up her courage. "Sarah Jane said that she saw you going out on an errand last night at midnight."

"Why would she want to go and say something like that? I was home in bed, where I should have been." Amilou looked sideways at Korine. "What're you doing, gossiping with that biddy anyhow?"

Korine's stomach churned. "She got me by the lemonade and started in. You know how she is."

"And *she* knows how *you* are. You know a sight more about people in this town than she'll ever know, and that hurts her." Amilou propped one foot up on the small table in front of her. "I don't understand people like that, making up stories and passing them along."

The creak from the opening of the screen door gave Korine a welcome interruption. She had felt awful enough mentioning the incident to Amilou. She felt even worse now, almost certain that Amilou had lied to her. Ruthlessly, Korine shoved the traitorous thought away. She knew Amilou. There was no way that her friend could kill anyone.

"The food in your dining room will feed this town for weeks," Janey said as she let the door swing shut behind her and rejoined the two women sitting on the quiet porch. For a few moments, the three women were silent. They'd exhausted pretty nearly every available subject before Amilou had gone back inside, except the one Korine now wished she hadn't brought up.

When she spoke again, Janey's voice was flustered: "I just got off the phone with J. J. He's on his way over here."

"Why?" Amilou put her untouched sandwich down on the plate. "J. J.'s not going to arrest me, is he?"

"No. Well, not really. He wants to ask you a few more questions. Evidently something else turned up that complicates things."

"Don't keep it to yourself. What things?" Korine demanded.

"He wouldn't tell me." Janey sounded miserable at having to be the go-between for her husband and her friend.

"Janey, you're not doing this, J. J. is. And he's just doing his job," Amilou said. She looked down at the napkin in her lap that she'd pleated into oblivion. "As much as I hate to admit this after all Greg did to me, I still loved him. I want whoever did this to him caught and punished." Hesitantly, she pulled her attention away from her lap and leaned forward in her chair. "Since I didn't harm Greg, I'd appreciate any help you can give me."

Janey's anguished look was all the answer Amilou got. Korine took refuge in her sandwich, avoiding being drawn into the discussion. Her first reaction was to press Janey to help Amilou, but that didn't seem fair when she had just questioned her friend's actions her own self. Korine had a lot to digest before she could trust herself to speak.

The women sat for a moment, watching the lightning bugs come out. When a car with a muffler problem pulled in and parked, all three leaned forward to see around the corner. A couple got out of the Nova and walked up the front steps. In unison, all three women ducked back again out of sight.

"That's Reverend Parker," Amilou said. "I don't think I can handle it if he offers me his condolences."

"I'll go ask Nicki to take care of him. Perhaps you're too distraught to see anyone?" Janey hinted delicately.

"That man told me it was my fault that Greg left. I *will* be distraught if I have to come face-to-face with him right now." Amilou smiled with gratitude at Janey.

Another car pulled in, this one with lights on the top. A large form emerged from the car.

"J. J., over here," Amilou called.

J. J. changed direction and came up the side steps.

"Y'all finished the food yet?" He pointed to the sandwich Amilou was picking at.

"You know better than that," Korine said, standing. "Janey just said that we have enough food on that dining room table to feed the whole town. Come on in and we'll get you a plate."

"I'll go," Janey said, when J. J. hesitated. "I've got to way-lay Reverend Parker anyhow. You take my seat, honey. I'll bring you back some of Mrs. Hawkins's special funeral casserole."

J. J. didn't answer, but his eyes gleamed.

"Do I need to go get Chaz?" Korine asked.

"It might be useful," J. J. responded.

"In that case, you'd better get your own plate. I'm not leaving you here alone with Amilou."

"It's all right, I won't confess until y'all get back." Amilou's tone was strained, even if her words were not.

Korine looked sharply at Amilou. Amilou stretched her mouth in a parody of a reassuring smile, which was belied by the deepening lines between her brows. Korine hurried out to find Chaz.

Five minutes later Korine and Chaz flanked Amilou. J. J. looked uncommonly grave as he worked his bulk into a chair. Janey and Nicki were running interference inside, keeping curious guests from interrupting.

J. J. glanced sideways at Korine, but she was darned if she was going to budge. She gave him back a look that told him in no uncertain terms that if he was going to interrogate her friend, Korine was going to be there to keep things civil.

"Amilou, I'm sorry to have to keep bothering you like this, but there is something else that came up." J. J. stopped and looked uncomfortable.

Amilou sat and watched him.

"How well do you know Sally Tucker?"

"Better than I'd like to know the woman who ran off with my husband." Bitterness soaked Amilou's voice like chicory-laced coffee.

Chaz reached out and took Amilou's hand in his. When she tried to take it back, he held on and shook his head warningly. Korine suspected that it was more to be able to keep a rein on his client rather than to comfort her.

"Can we get to the point?" Chaz asked in his best lawyer voice.

"Were you aware that Ms. Tucker was expecting?"

Amilou's face crumpled. It took a good ten minutes, and both Chaz's and J. J.'s handkerchiefs, to get her tears back under control.

"That was unfair," Korine hissed at J. J. while Amilou was blowing her nose. "You know how long she tried to get pregnant."

"Yes, I do know. But I had to find out if she knew about Sally."

"Satisfied?"

A stony stare was his notion of a reply.

"So you've talked to her at the Depot?" Amilou asked.

J. J. frowned. "You knew where she's staying?"

Chaz raised one eyebrow. "I've been tracking Greg's spending habits so that my client could recover as much of her assets as possible. Is there a problem with that?"

J. J. looked sour, as though the food on the plate Janey had handed him wasn't sitting well. "Possibly."

"Well? You found Sally. Did she confess to killing Greg?" Amilou asked.

If it was at all possible, J. J. became even sourer looking. "Not exactly."

"But you talked to her?" Amilou spoke to him slowly, seeming to recognize in mid-sentence that she and J. J. were not on the same page. "You said you found her. Don't tell me you haven't put her through the same hell you've given me today."

"I can't," J. J. answered. "Her place was vandalized, and Sally's missing. At this point, I don't even know if she's dead or alive."

Amilou's breath hissed as she drew it in past gritted teeth. Korine leaned over and put her hand on Amilou's arm. Korine could see Amilou's calf muscles tense as she pressed herself into the back of the chair. For a moment, Korine forgot her longtime friendship with J. J. and hated him for treating their friend this way.

Forcing her eyes open, Amilou expressed her opinion. "Damn—blast and thunderation." Amilou altered what she was about to say as Janey came back out onto the porch, portable phone in hand.

"What?" Janey asked.

"Sally's pregnant," Amilou said. "Her place was burgled, and she's taken off, who knows where."

The phone hit J. J. on the head as it dropped from Janey's hand.

"Oh, honey, I'm so sorry." Janey reached down and retrieved the phone from the floor. "Chaz, I know this isn't a good time, but Dennis is on the phone for you."

"I'll have to call him back," Chaz said.

"He said it was an emergency."

Chaz and Korine exchanged a look of concern. "I can only handle one emergency at a time. Mom, can you take it?"

Korine unfolded herself from the chair and took the receiver from Janey. "Dennis? Chaz can't come to the phone right now. How can I help?" She walked down the steps to the diminutive weeping cherry that Amilou, Janey, and Korine had planted to commemorate the opening of Three Dirty Women.

Korine only half-heard Dennis's tale of Katie Anne's flight from home. They'd had some dustup, which wasn't all that surprising what with the events of the day. Korine didn't even feel a hint of satisfaction that Dennis sounded disgusted with Susannah's lack of helpfulness.

Finally, after his repeated requests to speak with Chaz on the matter, Korine managed to reassure Dennis that she was certain that Katie Anne would come home. Amused in spite of the situation unfolding on the porch, she wondered when

Dennis had taken to turning to Chaz for advice on his love life. It had long been a sore spot in her life that the two young men didn't get along better than they did. Perhaps if Chaz had still been living at home when Korine took Dennis in, they might have grown up closer.

From the relative obscurity of the yard, Korine could still see the hunted look on Amilou's face. She looked from one to another of her friends sitting on the porch with her. The expression on her face when she looked at Janey startled Korine. Plainly, Amilou was wary of her friend and partner. Korine hoped that Amilou knew she could count on her. They'd been friends for fifteen years, ever since Korine and Charlie moved back to town.

J. J. was his same old self. Competent, but Pine Grove hadn't had a murder in years. Korine wondered if he would look beyond the obvious suspect. For Amilou's own sake, she certainly hoped so.

More worrisome, Janey's skin had developed a grayish cast, like she had been anointed with ashes. Her soft brown eyes were wide in disbelief. Korine frowned. Surely Janey wasn't beginning to doubt Amilou. J. J. adored his wife. Janey could be the influence that swung things in Amilou's favor. Or not.

Korine's feet left imprints of evening dew on the painted board steps as she returned to the porch. "Sorry about that. Dennis says he needs to talk to Chaz about the women in his life." She returned the phone to Janey. Chaz wrinkled his nose. Korine felt her mouth relax into a slight smile under his reassuring gaze.

Transferring that same reassuring gaze to his client, Chaz rolled up the cuffs of his white linen shirt. Amilou relaxed under the warmth of Chaz's look. His ability to communicate assurance never ceased to amaze Korine. She felt very proud to be his mother.

"I really am going to have to ask y'all to step inside," J. J. said to Korine and Janey. "I need to speak to Amilou alone, with Chaz, of course." J. J., who had been in no hurry before, finally got down to business. He took a handheld tape recorder out of his pocket and set it on the arm of his chair. "Go on now, girls," J. J. said encouragingly. "This would be easier to do here, than back down at the office."

"You're too kind," Amilou said dryly. "Go on," she agreed, making shooing motions with her hands. "Would you mind getting me a few hundred brownies, though? I'll eat them when J. J. has finished with me again."

Janey pushed a reluctant Korine toward the door. "We'll be inside," she said.

"We're heavy on potato salad." Korine turned to find Lorraine standing behind Janey and her in the doorway to the dining room.

"Isn't that always the way. People bring what's on hand, and potatoes were on sale last week. I've got a bag myself sitting at home." Korine paused delicately. "Is Reverend Parker still here?"

"No. He and his wife dropped off a pitiful plate of store-bought cookies and left when I told them that Miss Amilou was busy talking to Chief Bascom."

"I'll bet they did," Korine muttered. Having gotten what they came for, they would no doubt waste little time spreading sordid rumors around town.

The timer sounded from the kitchen. Lorraine turned to go. "I'm at least making some biscuits to go with the ham that Chaz brought."

Korine bit her tongue. She knew there was plenty of food in that kitchen, but telling Lorraine not to cook when someone had died was like trying to turn the tide. She felt it was her place to run the kitchen at this house, even if Amilou had run out of money for things like a full-time housekeeper. It was kind of her to be here. Korine left it alone.

"Did you know that Greg and Sally were back?" Janey asked Korine after Lorraine's muttered complaints about the sad state of modern funereal cuisine were replaced by the banging of pots and pans in the kitchen.

"I did see someone in town the other day going into the courthouse who could have been Sally. I'd heard she and Greg were back in town. I mentioned it to that young officer,

Leon, but he sailed right past the subject of Sally Tucker."

"I saw Sally on Wednesday," Janey said. "She and Amilou had words."

Korine stared at her. This was not news she wanted to hear. "Do you know what they were arguing about?"

"Sally came in and had her hair done the same time I was having a trim. She was awful. Bragging about what she'd done to Amilou's marriage. Talking about moving in here to The Pines as though it was a done deal."

"Was she with Greg?"

"All I know was that he wasn't at the Cut 'n Curl, Korine. Sally went on for the longest time about breaking up Amilou's marriage and taking The Pines away from her."

"Why on earth did Sally think she'd be moving in here?"

"I don't know. Amilou came in right when Sally said that the first thing she would do is paint the porch bright orange. Amilou lit into her. Said that house is about all she has left, thanks to Greg and Sally." Janey's eyes sparkled with unshed tears. "She told Sally that she'd die, or see Sally in . . ." Janey paused and cleared her throat. "Well, you know where, before she'd let her set a foot inside The Pines."

"Did you tell J. J. about this?"

Janey nodded. She studied the worn oriental runner under their feet. "Is it possible Amilou—"

Korine cut her off. "No."

"I don't like to think anyone I know well is capable of murder, but I've been there. If I hadn't gotten help when I was married to Raynell, I hate to think what I would have done to save myself. Everyone has a point at which they become capable of murder."

"Don't you dare compare Amilou with Raynell. When he beat you, Amilou didn't hesitate a minute in helping pay for your protection."

"I wasn't comparing Amilou to Raynell."

Korine felt her eyes open wide with surprise.

Janey continued, "You never told me that Amilou helped me back then." She raised one slim hand in protest.

"You didn't need to know. You needed help getting out of

an abusive marriage; Amilou had the means to give it to you. You'd only been in town a few days, but to her, it didn't matter." Korine could feel her blood pressure creeping up again.

Janey's eyes filled with tears. "I can't help what I saw, Korine. What with Sally talking about the house, and Amilou saying she'd kill before she let Sally and Greg into The Pines. Greg is dead. It doesn't look good."

"That's where we come in. Or should, at any rate," Korine responded. "You picked quite a time to decide to let loose all those negative things you've been holding back from us all this time. J. J. has to find the guilty person, or else my friend—and yours—is going to go to jail for something she could never do."

"J. J. won't put her in jail unless there's good reason to do so. Why are you so mad at me, anyhow? It's not my fault that Amilou's in the middle of this." Janey reached out one shaking hand to the wall as if to hold herself up.

Korine took a few deep breaths. On the third breath, her temper subsided. For the first time she realized that the lines on Janey's face reflected the same worry that Korine felt.

"I'm sorry," Korine said. "I'm spitting mad at the situation and you're getting the brunt of it."

Lorraine bustled through, disdainfully holding a silver plate filled with the store-bought goods from the Reverend. "Folks just don't know what's fitting for a funeral," she muttered, placing the offending tray on the far side of the table. The timer sounded from the kitchen, and she hurried past the pair in the hall.

When Janey spoke, she changed the subject entirely: "I hate to ask, but what are we going to do about Susannah's yard?"

"Finish the thing, I suppose," Korine replied. "I think we'd best do it without Amilou. Do you think we could ask Nicki?"

"I promised J. J. that I'd go on home soon. Can you ask her and let me know?" Janey slid her purse strap onto her shoulder. Plunging her hand into the bottom of the abyss within, she pulled out her keys. "Call me, won't you?"

Korine nodded. "As soon as I've heard something. I'll call

the Harrisons and tell them we'll start there on Monday."

"Make it Tuesday. Remember that J. J. said Amilou can try to have the funeral on Monday."

"Sounds good."

Janey walked out the door, closing it gently behind her. Korine watched her go down the steps and out the gates. Against her will, Korine found herself thinking again about Sarah Jane's assertion that Amilou had been out late the night before.

"Penny for them." Nicki's husky voice came from behind her.

"You don't want to know."

"Korine Sinclair McFaile, I've known you long enough to learn that the expression on your face means one thing: trouble for whoever crossed your path going the wrong direction. I believe you know the chief of police in this town? J. J. can handle it. Leave it alone."

"I will. As long as he goes in the right direction," Korine answered with a smile. "Janey and I were wondering if you could help finish up at Susannah's."

"Sure, as long as you promise not to drop a railroad tie on my arm again," Nicki said with a smile. "Now, who's staying with Amilou tonight?"

"Nobody needs to stay with me." Amilou's voice came from the doorway. "J. J. says he's not going to arrest me for a few days." She smiled slightly. "Besides, Greg's been gone a month. I've had some time to get used to doing without him."

Korine stared back at her friend. Remembering how many times Amilou had dissolved in tears throughout the day, she didn't really believe the brave words.

"Truly." Amilou picked up Nicki's pink bag and handed it to her. "It's funny, but I never feel lonely in this house."

Nicki gave Korine a look that Korine couldn't interpret. Then she leaned forward and kissed Amilou on the cheek. "I'll be by tomorrow."

Korine, Chaz, and Lorraine helped Amilou cram as much of the food in the fridge as they could, then wrapped the rest up tight. Lorraine's daughter arrived to give her a ride home about the same time Korine shouldered her purse.

Chaz and Korine walked out together to his Suburban, leaving Amilou alone in The Pines. If anyone had asked, Korine would have said that a tumbledown old house was cold comfort when compared to the companionship of friends. It troubled her that Amilou seemed content with it.

CHAPTER SEVEN

GRAVEL CRUNCHED BENEATH THE TIRES of Chaz's Suburban as they turned into the long lane to Korine's house. He took it a little too fast rounding the last curve. Korine winced. There was a distinct scraping noise as the fender brushed against a narrow portion of the towering hedge. Who was she to sit in judgment on Susannah's yard? Like the proverbial plumber and his leaky pipes, Korine's own yard needed tending.

After parking the car in front of the house, the two of them mounted the wooden steps to the front porch. Korine was tired to death. All she wanted to do was climb the stairs and fall into bed.

Then Chaz's anxious voice came from behind her. "Can you sit a while with me?"

She turned from unlocking the door and tried to see the expression on his face. The shadows foiled her. Hanging her purse on the front doorknob, Korine dropped into the closest chair. She shifted her balance as the split-cane seat jabbed her leg through the thin protection of her pants. Chaz took his place opposite her in the companion rocker.

"It would be helpful if Amilou had an alibi," Chaz finally said.

"You surely don't think she did it?"

"Of course not, Mom. But she's got the strongest motive. An alibi would be helpful."

"What about Sally? Amilou said that Greg wanted to come home. Wouldn't that make Sally a suspect."

"Sure. And the fact that she seems to be hiding makes that a stronger possibility. The problem is, we won't know Sally's side of the story until J. J. finds her. And with so few men at his beck and call, that might take a while."

Korine hesitated, then decided Chaz needed to know. "Janey told me that Amilou and Sally had a rather large public fight Wednesday morning."

"Amilou told me."

Korine felt a large burst of pent-up breath escape.

Chaz smiled at her. "She didn't do it, you know."

"Of course not! But as you said, I was starting to think that an alibi might be the only thing that would save her." Korine hesitated again, then continued, "Amilou was out late Thursday night."

"Late? How late?" Chaz's tone was sharp.

"Midnight late. She came by here with those preliminary plans around nine, but you remember how distracted she was. Sarah Jane said that she saw her driving out about midnight."

"Well, if she'd just had to throw Greg out—and the timing is about right for that—then she would have been distracted when she was here, but the second trip . . ." Chaz pressed his forefinger to his lips and looked away over the lawn. His chair creaked as he began to rock slowly back and forth.

Korine absorbed this. Amilou had told him about the fight with Sally at the Cut 'n Curl but hadn't told him that she was out late that night. Worse, she had out and out lied to Korine. Pressing her lips together, she looked out over her lawn and rocked slowly back and forth. Amilou had lied to her. Korine was doubly glad that she had apologized to Janey. Perhaps Janey did know better than anyone how much—or how little—it took to drive someone to murder.

A faint movement in the shadows at the far end of the porch materialized into Coco, the fluffy tortoiseshell cat who had adopted Korine several years before. She stepped daintily, her tail flying high behind her like a standard. In her mouth was a still-struggling mouse. Coco dropped her prize proudly at Korine's feet, where it promptly shot off the edge of the porch into the bushes beyond. Korine could almost see Coco roll her eyes. Turning her back on the temptation to leap after the fleeing prey, Coco flopped down at Chaz's feet and rolled over onto her back, swatting with one paw at his pant leg.

Korine cleared her throat. "You wanted to talk to me."

"Yes," Chaz said and leaned over and picked up the cat, who settled in. Her satisfied purr sounded like an outboard motor. "When I said that it would be good if Amilou had an alibi, I wondered if you might help us there."

Korine looked at her son, aghast. "Surely . . ."

"Mother! Despite all those horrid jokes about my profession, I am not dishonest. I don't want or need you to lie. But you know everyone, and people talk to you. Amilou needs your help. I'm merely asking you to do what comes naturally to you: Be nosy."

"Chaz!" Try as she might, Korine couldn't make her tone sharp enough to hide her relief.

Korine's son grinned unrepentantly. "Amilou needs you right now. You are the single best listener in Pine Grove. All I'm asking is that you use your talent to her benefit." He held his hand out in warning. "I'm not asking you to do anything that will get you into trouble with J. J. or with whoever did kill Greg. Listening only. Don't run all over town trying to establish an alibi for Amilou. I don't want you to become a target."

Korine looked at her son with renewed respect. She knew that he was grown, it just slipped her mind from time to time. He had earned the esteem of his clients, she owed him at least that much.

"Did you call Dennis back?" Korine said, suddenly remembering her nephew's earlier panicked phone call.

"Not yet. What did he want now?" Chaz asked. As usual, his tone was barely civil when he talked about his younger cousin. Chaz had been in college when Charlie died. Something had happened between the two boys on Chaz's first visit home after Korine had taken Dennis in. Whatever it was—and neither boy would discuss it with her—had driven a wedge between them that Korine couldn't seem to dislodge. When she'd asked Chaz the last time, he'd said point-blank that it was none of her business.

"Is Katie Anne doing all right?" Chaz finally asked.

"She's run off. That's what Dennis was so upset about."

"I'll go give him a call," Chaz said rising. For a moment though, he didn't move. Placing a hand softly on Korine's shoulder, he said, "You can't carry all of us, you know. You may have to pick and choose."

Before Korine could ask Chaz what he meant by that, he'd turned and gone back in the house. The cane seat sank half an inch beneath her as she settled back in the rocker. Coco jumped lightly up into her lap and curled up under her hand. Korine settled her elbows on the wide arms of the chair and looked out over the painted railing.

Even in the dusk you could see that the pattern of overgrowth threatening the drive was also taking over the front lawn. Korine's garden had been featured in several magazines. You'd never know it now. She spent all her time weeding other people's retreats and had very little energy left for her own. Still, there was a rough beauty to the property. It made a good contrast to the ordered rows she hoed in other people's yards.

"I'm sorry, what did you say?" Korine said in response to a murmured question from Chaz. He took the chair opposite her once again.

His deep voice repeated, "Are you all right?"

She looked up to meet his questioning look. "I'll be fine," Korine said firmly. "Thank you, by the way, for getting Amilou out so quickly."

"Getting innocent people out of jail isn't very hard. But, you're welcome." Chaz doffed an imaginary hat. "Mom, this may be a funny time to ask, but something Dennis said today got me to wondering again. Why did Aunt Callie take off all those years ago and leave Dennis and his dad?"

"Marrying into the McFaile family isn't as easy as it looks."

"If marrying into the McFaile family is so hard, why didn't you walk out?"

"Your father was an exception to the McFaile rule. Besides, Callie wasn't as strong as the Sinclairs. I had an advantage."

"Being a McFaile myself, remind me never to ask you for a letter of reference."

"You're too like your father to need one."

"Thanks, I think." Chaz brushed a speck of dust from his wing tips.

"Is Dennis okay?"

"He went out after Katie Anne."

"I guess he'll be late, then. I won't wait up." Korine stood and walked into the bright hallway. The small cherry drop-leaf table by the door was buried under a pile of mail. She had meant to go through it all today and pay her bills. They wouldn't wait much longer. She put her hand out to scoop them up, then pulled it back. She was much too tired to do anything about them now. Turning her back on duty, she mounted the steps to her bedroom.

"Loitering?" J. J. roared. "Come again?" He'd picked up the phone in his office when he was finally on his way home for the night.

"Katie Anne Graham, sir," Jett Merriweather repeated. "She says she's lost something and was looking for it. What should I do? The lady of the house is pretty upset."

"I'll be right over. Give me the address."

J. J. scribbled the address on a scrap of paper and went out to his car. The drive over was pretty uneventful, although Leon did screech out of the apartments over on Teasdale Drive as J. J. drove past. He wished that Leon had been hot on Sally Tucker's trail instead of out for a night with his girlfriend. He couldn't afford to work his officers twenty-four hours a day, but it bothered him that they hadn't caught up with Sally.

Turning left onto Treeline Drive, J. J. coasted to a stop in front of a brightly lit McMansion that had gone up a few years ago when the Junker farm was sold. A very miserable-looking Katie Anne sat, handcuffed, on the front stoop. An irate matron stood over her with her fists on her hips.

"This would never happen in Atlanta!" she shrilled. "Our police there know how to treat criminals."

"Good evening, ma'am," J. J. spoke softly, letting his deep voice rumble in his chest. "What seems to be the problem here?"

"This . . . this . . . girl was snooping outside our windows during our party! She must be casing our house for a burglary. That's been happening so much lately. And with that murder . . ."

Katie Anne shuddered and began to cry. J. J. indicated that Jett should take her and put her in J. J.'s cruiser.

"Well, ma'am," J. J. began again in his best aw-shucks style. "I'm sure you were pretty upset. But that girl has had one heck of a day. You'll have to excuse her behavior. It was her house where the body was found, and she was supposed to be gettin' married there tomorrow."

"I see," the matron said frostily. "You're going to cover it up. I will speak to the mayor's wife in the morning about this. Sarah Jane'll see you take action." She stepped back inside her house and slammed the door. J. J. winced, waiting for the lintel to fall, but it stayed put.

He walked back down the path to the gate and let himself out. Walking over to the car, he placed one hand on the roof and leaned down to look in the backseat.

"Could you use a hot cup of coffee?" he asked the girl sitting quietly inside wringing her hands.

Katie Anne looked up at him, eyes round. "You're not going to arrest me?"

"Not unless you tell me you really were planning to rob that woman. If you were, I'd tell you to save your energy. Women like her never have anything but fake jewelry. Not like that big engagement ring Dennis bought you."

Katie Anne burst into tears again.

J. J. shut the door and straightened up. "Jett, you did right by calling me."

"Thanks." The young man sketched a salute and ambled back to his car.

J. J. climbed in and turned the key. Easing out, he pointed the car toward the Green Whistle. Even though it was nearly closing time, he knew Juanita June would run one more pot of coffee for him.

"Honey, what are you doing here the night of your

rehearsal dinner?" Juanita June asked as J. J. ushered Katie Anne into the bright diner. His nose twitched from the aroma of fresh-baked apple pie.

"I'm not getting married," Katie Anne replied.

"Can you put us somewhere quiet?" J. J. requested. "We need to talk."

"Your office burn down, J. J.?"

"You'd be the first to know it," J. J. retorted. They followed Juanita June to the far corner booth and sat down. "Katie Anne's had a rough day. I thought I'd help her calm down a little bit before taking her home."

Juanita June poured coffee into Katie Anne's mug and set it down in front of her.

"Thanks." Katie Anne wrapped her hands around the mug.

"If you don't mind telling me, what are you doing here?" Juanita June asked.

"I'm not getting married." To J. J.'s dismay, tears began to fall down Katie Anne's cheeks again. She grabbed a napkin from the dispenser at the end of the table and pressed it to her eyes.

"Don't jump to any conclusions, honey," Juanita June said. "What with all you've been through today, a lot of things will seem different, but Dennis and you not getting married? I can't see that."

J. J. tapped his finger on his mug, trying to get Juanita June to finish her business and leave the two of them alone so he could figure out what Katie Anne had been up to. Juanita June filled it up, then started to turn her attention back to Katie Anne.

"Oh hell," Juanita June said. "That Sylvester's got his cup in the air for more coffee. I'll be back in a minute."

Katie Anne raised the cup of coffee to her lips. She took a quick sip, then hastily put the mug down and grabbed another napkin. J. J. knew she was in bad shape if something as normal as hot coffee could bring on tears. Leaning her head against the plastic of the booth behind her, Katie Anne closed her eyes.

She'd spread her hands out on the table as if holding herself upright by pushing on it. The bare ring finger on her left hand caught J. J.'s eye.

"What's going on, Katie Anne?" J. J. asked when she opened her eyes again.

"I threw my ring in their yard, then went back for it." She picked up her mug and took a cautious sip.

"Threw your ring?!" J. J. asked incredulously.

"I know. That's what Dennis will say. If he ever speaks to me again."

"You want to talk about it?"

J. J. could see her backbone stiffen. "I'd rather not. It's private."

Juanita June came back to refill their cups. "By the way, who do I send the bill to, you or your officer?"

"I beg your pardon?"

"That skinny officer of yours—Leon?—blew through here a few minutes ago with his girlfriend. They hurled half my glassware at each other. Seems she was carrying on with Greg Whittier while she was engaged to Leon."

"He was sleeping with her, too?" Katie Anne's voice was breathless. "Dear sweet heaven above!"

Too? J. J. thought. His police antenna went up.

"Just what was your relationship with Greg Whittier?" he asked Katie Anne.

"He dated my mother," Katie Anne said sharply. She stuck her little chin in the air. Folding her arms across her chest, she proceeded to try and outstare a professional. No surprise, her gaze dropped first.

J. J. stood. "I'll take you home."

"That won't be necessary," Katie Anne said, her face settling into rebellious lines.

Juanita June stepped back out of the way as if she thought more glasses would be flying her way.

"Don't go poking around in that lady's yard for now, Katie Anne. I'll send someone over there tomorrow to have a look around."

"You handled that well, Chief Bascom," Juanita June said sarcastically, blocking his way out of the booth.

At the look on J. J.'s face, Juanita June's grin slid off her face.

"Send my office a bill for the glassware. I've got to follow that girl and make sure she gets home safely. We've got a killer on the loose." J. J. threw a few bills on the table to cover his coffee and stalked out after Katie Anne.

He didn't know whether to be sorry for that young girl or mad as hell that she'd pulled one over on him. How many women in Pine Grove had slept with the victim? If Greg weren't already dead, J. J. would be tempted to kill him.

CHAPTER EIGHT

EVEN WITH THE WEIGHT of the Saturday morning high school football pages between them, J. J. could feel Janey staring at him. She sat fidgeting on the other side of the kitchen table. Every now and again, she would set her coffee mug down with decided force. If she had something on her mind that was so all-fired important, why hadn't she come out with it before he picked up the paper?

J. J. dropped the crease of the newspaper three inches so that he could make eye contact with his wife. She looked guilty, like he'd caught her hiding more Tupperware in the cabinet when she already had enough to keep leftovers till Christmas.

"What?" he asked. His tone was almost cordial, for that time of day, especially after the night he'd had. J. J. hadn't arrived back home until nearly midnight after following Katie Anne home.

"I don't know," she finally answered him. "Nothing probably."

"What nothing?" J. J. sighed. The Guess-What-I'm-Thinking game had never been his favorite couple activity.

Janey got up and pulled an apple from the refrigerator. She swung her hip against the door to close it, then turned to rummage in the utensil drawer. Bending over the sink, she started to peel the apple.

Momentarily distracted, J. J. asked hopefully, "Are you making apple-cinnamon coffeecake for breakfast?" The thought of her mouthwatering cooking made him forget the paper. His team hadn't won anyway. He got up to help his wife. She slid the white casserole dish onto the top of the stove.

"Chopped or sliced?" Janey asked, knife poised above the half-pared apple.

"Sure," J. J. answered, distracted by the sight of Janey's hand clasping a knife identical to the one he'd picked up the day before. "Where'd you get that?"

"You turning into one of those penny-pinching husbands? I bought this through the band fund-raiser last year, before we got married." Janey gave him her enigmatic look, then turned her attention back to the apple. "They only sold four hundred of these, so they had to turn to fruit trees and light bulbs to earn enough money for the new uniforms."

"That a fact?"

"I know. Those kids worked so hard." Janey sliced the fruit into thin slices and put them in a saucepan. As they sizzled in the cooking oil, she finally made eye contact and registered the worry J. J. had all over his face. "What?"

"We own the identical twin of a knife I found yesterday—a knife I think is the murder weapon."

"Oh, my," Janey said, saucepan poised above the mixing bowl.

"Yes. Oh, my, indeed. Now I've got to figure out who it belonged to, how it came to be in the wrong place at the right time, and whose fingerprints were on it."

"And I've just told you that you've got four hundred solid citizens to choose from."

"Yep. Thanks, honey, for your help," J. J. said with a smile. "You wouldn't happen to know where Sally Tucker is? Really make my day if you could save me the trouble now of finding her."

Janey picked up her mug and hid behind it as she took a sip.

"What?" J. J. asked.

"Nothing." Janey emerged from behind the cup. Far from the grin J. J. had expected, she wore a frown of concentration. "It's not fair for me to pass on things that have no basis in fact."

"I'm your husband. How about you just tell me like it was pillow talk or something. I'll sort out if it's important or not."

"No," Janey said, avoiding his eyes as she turned on the mixer.

"What do you mean, no? If you know something, you have to share it with me." J. J.'s mug thumped the table as he set it down.

"I don't have to share my intuitions and feelings with you, even if we *are* married." Janey had scrunched her face up, as if trying not to cry.

He'd had to fight his natural inclination to give in to her when Janey began to cry in Susannah's kitchen the day before. For the sake of the investigation he again found the nerve to resist the temptation to let it be. "Honey, if you know something, tell me. I'm usually pretty good at sifting out what's chaff and what's wheat. But I can't do any sifting to find the truth if nobody tells me anything."

He got up to pour himself another cup of coffee. The more he thought about this case, the more frustrated he got. "I find what I think is the murder weapon close to where the body was stashed at Susannah's, who is trying on the helpless-female nonsense. The murder weapon turns out to be one of God-knows-how-many hundreds of knives everyone in town owns, instead of something I might be able to identify easily. Amilou, who has the best motive to kill Greg, is sitting in her house all stiff and red-eyed, like she was a real widow or something. Korine's like as not to snap my head off if I go near her friend. Sally Tucker—my own personal favorite suspect—is still missing. Greg slept with nearly every woman in town, evidently including Katie Anne Graham and her mother. And to top it off, my wife's having intuitions, which she won't share with me because I might get all confused."

J. J. returned and stood next to the table, too frustrated to sit. He slammed the flat of his hands on the table. His voice rose. "Hell, I *am* confused. Why that means people think I can't work it out, I don't know."

Janey stared at J. J., her pupils wide and fixed. He swore silently and got up to put his arms around his wife. "Honey, I'm sorry." He rocked her back and forth in his arms. "I'm sorry," he crooned over and over.

Janey fought him at first. She always did. He never knew when a small lapse into anger on his part would trigger one of these episodes. It hadn't happened for almost six months. But when it did, Janey sank into an inner hell J. J. couldn't begin to imagine. The first time he saw it, he had been scared to death.

About the time that Janey and J. J. had started dating seriously, he lost his temper and punched a wall over some fool thing that had nothing to do with her. Despite knowing her history, he was still stunned by her reaction.

The normally placid woman he knew and loved had curled up into a ball. Crying, shaking, Janey was unable to let him near her to comfort her in any way. She told him afterward that the memories of Raynell rolled in like a heavy fog over her senses, rendering her unable to distinguish anything except that J. J. was male, and angry. That had been two years before. They had been through a lot in the time since then. Loving her as he did, he'd even promised not to swear in front of her. Usually, he remembered.

A very long half hour later, Janey took a shuddering breath and let it out. She was back. Clinging to him, she cried for a minute longer. Straightening, she pushed her hands through her hair.

"Honey, I'm so sorry." J. J. tenderly cupped her smooth cheek.

Janey pushed herself up. Her hands shook against the table as she stood beside him. He wished with all his heart that he could break all his bad habits. "You're just a man, J. J. Don't expect more of yourself than anyone else. I'm sorry too. You deserve a wife who won't fall apart on you."

"Don't you dare blame yourself for this." J. J. slid his hand up Janey's bare arm, feeling the softness of the downy hair bend beneath his fingertips. "Raynell is the one to blame."

She put her arms around him and pressed her face into his shoulder. Slowly, the trembling stopped. Janey lifted her head and pulled back so that her brown eyes could meet his searching gaze.

"Are you O.K.?"

"Better. One of these days . . ."

"So you up to answering questions?" J. J. peered down at his wife, gauging her reaction.

"You." Janey said, pushing at J. J.'s chest. "The things you'll do to soften up a witness." She looked down and twisted the top button on his shirt for moment, then spoke again. "I'm willing to swear that Amilou didn't know he was buried in that bed." She placed a finger over J. J.'s lips as he started to ask a question. "No, don't interrupt me, or I'll never get it out. She was surprised, J. J.—genuinely so—when she uncovered Greg's hand."

"But?"

"Something's not right with her. She's afraid of something. Keeping something buried inside. I know what it feels like. I can tell when somebody else is doing it."

"Do you think she killed him and got someone else to dispose of the body?"

"I don't think so. The only person she'd ever ask to do anything would be Korine. Can you see Korine burying a body?"

"Some days, yes."

"No, you can't." Janey mock-pushed J. J.'s chest away.

"Okay, I'll give you that Susannah still loved Greg," he said. "But can you see Susannah ever keeping it together long enough to kill him, then cart his dead body across the lawn and bury him?"

Janey shook her head. "I'll admit that Amilou's been acting odd the last few days. For example, it took her forever when she left to get fertilizer from Klein's hardware for us yesterday morning. Said she couldn't find it, like she couldn't pick it up blindfolded once she got in the door or something. Still, I'm willing to swear she was in shock—and genuinely grieving—over Greg's death."

Janey paused and drew a shuddering breath. J. J. tightened his arms around her protectively. "You okay?"

"Sure," Janey said, denying what J. J. knew must have been residual emotion from her earlier fit. "Looks to me like you need to talk with Sally. I told you that she and Amilou got into it last Wednesday."

"Believe me, I remember."

"Well, Korine saw Sally going into the courthouse earlier that day. I've been trying to figure out if that had anything to do with Sally's thinking she could get her hands on The Pines."

J. J. stroked Janey's arm. "Sally never struck me as someone you'd toss your life away for. Greg was executor of Judge Pierce's will. What if he found something that made Sally more attractive to him?"

"What are you saying?"

"Sally Tucker's mother was an especially good 'friend' of Judge Pierce's after Amilou's mother died. What if the Judge left something substantial to Sally in memory of Maybelle when he died? Something Amilou didn't want to give her. That would account for the fact that Greg chose Sally over all the other women in his life."

"The Pines?" Janey's voice rose. "Sounds like you need to make a trip to the courthouse come Monday morning." She touched the pulse on J. J.'s throat with the tip of her finger. "Does this make up for the knife?" she asked.

He twirled one of his wife's long curls around his forefinger. "Maybe, honey." He laid his cheek next to Janey's and slid his hands down her back, pulling her closer. "But I can think of something that definitely would."

J. J. felt like the phone was welded to his ear. The cheerful Saturday-morning voices of the big-city radio disk jockeys grated on his nerves. He'd already finished looking through the report of the activity from the night before. (One B&E he knew about, one he didn't, and one drunk and disorderly. Four traffic stops. Katie Anne's trespassing call.) By the time he finished waiting for the state crime lab to pick up their phone and then ambled down the hall, the pot of coffee he'd put on before making the call would have boiled dry. He stretched out an arm and turned the desk clock toward him. Nine o'clock. Ten minutes on hold, long distance no less.

"Hello?" The tinny voice of the lab tech scraped across J. J.'s nerves.

"Yes?" he answered. "This is J. J. Bascom, looking for the results on a murder weapon I sent down there yesterday."

"Yesterday?" There were rustlings of paper in the background. "From where?"

"Pine Grove. Greer County."

"Oh, yes, I remember now. The ME told us to wait on that one. She's got another serial killer down here . . ."

"I don't care what that blasted woman told you. I need to ID a murder weapon. At least tell me if it matched the victim's blood sample."

"The blood types on the knife, let's see . . ."

J. J. spoke over the sound of paper shuffling as he repeated, "Types? As in plural?"

"Yeah. Do you know how many murderers leave their blood type on the knife? Amazingly stupid, most of 'em."

"So did we have a match with the victim?" J. J. broke in.

"We only did preliminary tests, but yeah, you got a match. It'll take a while to get the full range back, but . . . hang on a minute." There was a click followed by the annoying sound of the radio announcer. J. J. took the phone away from his ear and treated it to one of his nastier looks.

"Hello?" The harried female voice came back on the line.

"Yes?" J. J. said.

"Sorry. My husband wanted to know when I was coming home so he could go fishing. My next off shift looks like it'll happen about next year."

J. J. greeted this sally with silence.

"That's what passes for humor around here."

"I got it. Can you do a breakdown on the other type also?"

"Sure. I'll be here all night anyhow." The woman sounded as harassed as J. J. felt.

"Thank you." J. J. tried to put more enthusiasm in his voice, but it came out sounding flat. "I do appreciate it."

"Bad up there?" She detected the weariness in his voice.

"The victim is the husband of a friend." He dragged his attention back to the matter at hand.

"Your weekend's going to be worse than mine then. I've got one good set of prints and a partial. I'll keep my fingers crossed that you pull in a match. I'll try to remember to call you with any further results before you have to call me."

"Thanks." This time J. J. meant it. "What's your name again?"

"Esther Patton."

"Thanks, Esther, you're a doll." He hung up the phone and headed for the coffee. Once he got there, he poured two cups and headed back to see if the fax had come through.

"Marlene?"

"Yes, sir?" Marlene's voice came from under the desk.

"What are you doing under there?"

"I lost something." Her voice had the curt, don't-even-ask tone that J. J. had learned meant business.

"Do you have a full report on that second B&E from last night?"

"Jett got that one," she answered, still doubled over in her desk chair. "The folks dropped the charges when Jett got there. It was really a domestic disturbance."

"Well . . ."

"Would you leave me alone, already?!" Marlene said, still under her desk. "Something just came in over the fax. Weren't you waiting for it?"

"I'll call Jett," J. J. said, backing down again from his receptionist. He knew he was supposed to be in charge of his own office, but Marlene was more than he could handle on three hours' sleep.

Shutting the door firmly behind him to keep something solid between him and the dispatcher, J. J. sat in his chair and swiveled to look out the window. He hadn't talked to half the people he needed to in this case. He wasn't even sure where to begin. Closing his eyes, he tried to prioritize his thoughts.

Marlene buzzed through on the intercom line. "Chief, I've got a call coming in on a disturbance in the Green Whistle. Juanita June says that Sally Tucker just came in."

J. J. felt his mouth twist in a smile as he reached over and picked up the phone. "Tell Juanita June to keep her there until I can get over there. She has my permission to sit on that young lady if she has to."

J. J. slammed his finger on the cutoff button and hitched himself up out of his chair. Reaching for his hat, he strode out of the room and down the hall toward the door. As he passed Marlene's desk, he saw her bend over the trash can again—still looking for her lost item. Whatever she had lost, it must be pretty important to her.

This is going to make one epic story for the gossips in Pine Grove, was J. J.'s first thought as he walked in the door of the Green Whistle. Glass crunched underfoot like country road gravel. Sally Tucker and a young woman J. J. knew he should know faced off in the center of the restaurant. Juanita June was as angry a woman as J. J. had ever seen, fists on hips, brows drawn together to form one threatening line above hard eyes. Her exhortation to the two women to stop breaking all the glassware in the Green Whistle was doing as much good as teaching pigs to fly.

J. J. strode over, trying to get around Leon, who struggled ineffectively to separate the two women. Leon reached in and grabbed the not-Sally young woman, swinging her around to face him. Sally seized that opportunity to slam her purse down on the top of her opponent's head.

Like dominoes, the girl folded onto Leon, who went over backwards onto J. J., who hit the floor with a bone-jarring crash, very effectively neutralizing their attempts to take Sally into custody. Emerging from under his officer, J. J. saw Sally's blue eyes open wide as she recognized him. Stepping daintily over the men sprawled under the unconscious woman, she ran lightly out the door. By the time J. J. climbed to his feet, he heard the squeal of tires in the parking lot outside.

"Next time, grab the right woman when you're out on an arrest," J. J. said to Leon. Belatedly, J. J. realized that the unconscious girl on the floor was Claudia, Leon's girlfriend. "Oh, get Claudia over to the hospital."

J. J. turned and walked out, too frustrated to even say so much as thank you, much less apologize for the further glass breakage to a now-speechless Juanita June. He found plenty to say to the deserted parking lot when he got outside, however. Climbing into his cruiser, he called Marlene.

"She got away," J. J. said in response to Marlene's question. "You'll have to ask Leon why. He's on the way over to Pickles to the hospital with Claudia."

At Marlene's exclamation, J. J. explained, "Evidently she was sleeping with Greg while she was engaged to Leon, so who knows what-all he's done to mess up this investigation. As near as I can tell from the bystanders' testimony, Claudia and Sally were going at it hammer and tongs over Greg."

There was a brief pause on the far end of the line, then Marlene said, "I'll call Jett and get him out there looking for Sally."

"Call over to Pickles. They offered me two overtime officers for this case. I guess I'm going to have to take them up on it. Between the three of them, somebody's bound to pick up Sally. I'm going back in here and see if Leon knows anything before he takes off with Claudia."

J. J. hauled himself out of the car and walked slowly back toward the Green Whistle. The worst thing that could happen would be that Leon hadn't gotten any information out of Sally before she scampered. At least that's what he thought before he opened the door and came face-to-face with a grinning Sylvester.

Half an hour later, J. J. drove out of the parking lot, a very large pocket-full of change poorer, having paid for Juanita June's glassware, his professional pride in shreds. Finding out publicly that Leon, his former top officer, hadn't been trying to apprehend Sally at all was beyond galling. Evidently, Leon had been following Claudia, who had arranged to meet Sally on her own. Neither Claudia nor Leon would say anything about that. The only bright spot in the conversation was that Leon wasn't on duty when all this occurred.

The pair of ex-lovers had deigned to part with the information that Claudia had gotten a phone call from Sally around six that morning, telling her to meet her in the Green Whistle for breakfast or 'she'd be sorry.' Claudia had gone—

not, she said, because she was afraid, but because she was curious. Before Sally could say a word, Leon had shown up, precipitating the argument resulting in Juanita June's call.

All of which left J. J. with zero knowledge of Sally's whereabouts during the time of the murder. J. J. amended his mental list. Claudia had also parted with the information that Sally had called Webber insurance about the policy before the body was found. That was pretty interesting. All he had to do now was get his hands on Sally and get a few other facts straight. J. J. made a mental note to call the phone company and tell them to hurry up and install Caller ID in their service area. It sure would have been nice to know where Sally had been when she called Claudia. As it was, all Sally left behind her was a smoke screen.

J. J. started the engine and headed out to talk with Susannah. It would be very interesting to know if she knew about her daughter's relationship with Greg Whittier. Now that he thought back, Susannah's denial had been a shade too firm concerning Greg and her daughter. Susannah was not above ruining her daughter's wedding if she had discovered that Katie Anne had been sleeping with her former lover.

It couldn't be helped, he thought, that Katie Anne's experience the night before would make her a more difficult witness this morning. Thinking again of the fact that Sally had checked to see if she could cash in on Greg's insurance policy before anyone else even knew he was dead might make this trip an unnecessary one. J. J. knew from experience, however, that solving any case included dotting his *i*'s and crossing his *t*'s. He pointed the car toward the Grahams' house and pressed the gas.

CHAPTER NINE

KORINE PUT HER WORK GLOVES on the shelf by the back door next to her garden snips. Pulling open the screen door, she went inside. At first light, she had been in the garden, deadheading the roses and weeding the kitchen garden. The early noise of commuter traffic sounded its morning call on the road down the hill.

It was time for the first cup of coffee of the day. Stirring in a dollop of milk, she picked up the phone and tried Amilou. The line was busy. Before she had shooed Korine out the door the night before, Amilou had mentioned wanting to work in a few more ideas on the Harrisons' garden design. Korine knew her friend well enough to know that design work served the same purpose for Amilou that weeding did for Korine: a constructive distraction from whatever trouble ailed her. Chances were, Amilou had stayed up all night and taken the phone off the hook.

Three Dirty Women, even if it was new to the business, was not simply a we'll-dig-in-your-dirt-for-you firm. While Korine's skills had been honed getting her yard ready for garden club meetings, and Janey had a superb eye for color, Amilou supplied professional credentials. She'd gotten a degree in botany in college and had gone back for several landscape architecture courses over the years. Most importantly, she was a darn fine designer.

Korine picked up the phone again, then put it back down. The oven clock said ten after eight. Plenty of time to get to the bills and still arrive at Amilou's before she was inundated with well-wishers. Chaz had left earlier, saying he needed to catch up on things at his office, and Dennis hadn't come in the night before. Korine could only assume that he and Katie

Anne had patched things up. He'd probably stayed over at Susannah's with Katie Anne.

Korine sat down at her desk and plowed her way through the bills, starting with the ones that would soon be due. She had slipped the last one into its envelope when the phone rang.

Without preamble, Amilou said, "You would not believe how rude some people are. I've gotten five calls from reporters asking me why I did away with my husband. They aren't even subtle."

"I can be there in about ten minutes." Korine checked her watch. "Who else can I call to come help?"

"Just you. I'm not up to anyone else. Make sure you come around back to get in. There's a couple of newspaper types out front. Funny, I don't know them at all, but they assume that they know all about me, and none of it good. It leaves me very happy that my grandfather thought to put in an eight-foot wrought-iron fence."

Amilou might have lost Greg, but she hadn't lost her sense of humor. Korine smiled with relief. "I'm on my way to help you hold down the fort."

"I'll buzz you in when you get here."

Korine nearly ran over a photographer on the way in. He was still lying on the ground where he'd thrown himself out of the way when the gate swung shut behind her car. She was so busy grinning in her rearview mirror that she had to hit the brakes to keep from crashing through the boxwood hedge lining the pull-through by the side door.

There was a woman standing outside the front gate. Korine's heart sank as she recognized the busybody that Sarah Jane Jenkins had gone over to talk with the night before. There was no telling what the biggest gossip in town had said to her; the fact that she carried a press card wouldn't matter one little bit to Sarah Jane.

As soon as Korine cracked her window and turned off the car, the woman began to shout: "Is Ms. Whittier going to turn herself in?"

The woman pressed her point: "Who do you believe killed Greg Whittier?"

Korine placed her foot on the first step up to the porch.

Then the woman asked, "How do you feel being best friends with a murderess?"

Korine turned and shaded her eyes with one hand. She took a steadying breath. Unable to resist the opportunity to get her own back at this insensitive reporter, Korine walked back toward the fence and looked the woman up and down before answering.

The questioner wore her powder blue suit like a store mannequin. You could dress them up . . . Already regretting reacting, but unwilling to retreat without having the last word, Korine asked, "Cast your mind about and see if you can't fix on the image of your best friend." Korine waited until the look of surprise was replaced by one of wariness on the woman's face. "Now see if you can picture your friend killing someone she loves."

The woman had enough grace to look uncomfortable before she shoved a card through the fence. "I know it's inconceivable, but we've had tips that—"

Korine let the card drop to the grass and ground it under the toe of her white sneaker. "Consider your sources," Korine said. "The people who know Amilou Whittier best know she didn't have anything to do with this." She spun on her heel and ran up the steps to the house.

Amilou let her in. Both of them stood in the cool of the hallway, shaking with emotion.

"How long has she been out there?"

"Since about six o'clock. This one's more persistent than the others. There were ten of them to begin with. Talk about your slow news days." A sheepish smile stole over Amilou's face. "I went out to get the paper. One of them even went so far as to climb the fence. It took him ten minutes to fall off once he got stuck. Fortunately for me, he fell on the right side of the fence, or I'd be nursing the idiot on my couch. That's his shirt over there." Amilou pointed out a fluttering rag on top of one of the spears in the corner.

"I suppose it could be worse." Korine was pleased to see Amilou's smile broaden as her quick mind completed the thought Korine had begun.

"The poor thing could have gotten stuck by the seat of his pants," they said in unison. Whooping with slightly hysterical laughter, they retired to the kitchen.

"Then we can turn the bed around this tree. It'll be lovely." Amilou used a darker green pencil to shade in the outline of the tree. She was right—with that combination of ferns and shade-tolerant color, it would be lovely. Korine just couldn't concentrate on the plans the way she usually could.

"Amilou," Korine began hesitantly. "Do you know if you have an alibi?"

"How can I have an alibi? We don't even know when he was killed. I wish people would quit asking me where I was. It reminds me too much of so many of my last conversations with Greg before he left." Amilou lapsed into a moody silence as she tapped the eraser against her cheek.

Her voice harsh, Amilou continued, "Toward the end, we didn't have conversations, we had grilling sessions. 'When will you be home, dear? When will we have time together, dear? Where is my trust fund, dear?'"

"Why do you suppose Greg wanted to come home?" Korine asked hesitantly. This bitterness reminded her too forcibly of just how little she really knew of Amilou's feelings for her husband.

"Maybe Chaz was getting uncomfortably close to finding evidence that Greg mishandled the estate." Amilou absently added a clump of forsythia that sabotaged the flowing lines she had inserted up until then. Korine started to object, then stopped when she saw the expression on Amilou's face. The distraction of working had worn off for her friend.

Amilou threw the pencil back in the wooden box she kept her supplies in and fished out a red one. "Even though they were two of a kind, I still can't believe Daddy left Greg in charge of my money." The lead snapped off the end of Amilou's pencil, leaving a splotchy red blur where a butterfly bush was meant to be.

Korine handed Amilou an eraser. "I wondered about that."

Amilou scrubbed the blotch with the eraser. "Not as much as I have. Daddy may have been positively medieval in his thinking, but this goes way beyond that. Greg must have been holding something over Daddy's head."

Korine digested the silence and changed the subject. "What did Chaz say when you told him about Sally?"

"What about her?"

"Sally was talking about moving into The Pines."

"Janey told you." Amilou's voice was strained.

"And you told Chaz. We're just worried about you. Janey's standing between her friend and her husband. It isn't much fun."

"Being suspected of killing Greg isn't any fun for me, either."

Stung by the note of accusation in Amilou's voice, Korine took a breath and said, "Janey and I don't think you did it. You know it doesn't matter what J. J. thinks personally, he's got to look at all the possibilities."

"Well, I don't like being a *possibility*."

"I don't blame you. I hate it too. That's why I want to help you if I can," Korine said, bewildered by the antagonism radiating from Amilou.

The two friends looked across the table at each other. So many years of friendship couldn't be denied. Amilou reached out. Korine met her halfway. They shook hands like schoolgirls making a secret pact.

Amilou gave Korine a squeeze, then let go and said, "I don't know what made Sally decide she needed my house as well as my husband. There was no way she could get her hands on this place. Daddy willed it directly to me. He had some sort of fight with his lawyer and drew up a holographic will, but even that old fuddy-duddy said it was perfectly clear that Daddy meant the house to go directly to me. It was just the money to keep it up that he tied up in that trust fund."

Amilou pushed herself up from the table and went over to look out the window. "I got a second opinion from Chaz about it. He said it was all legal, even though the damn thing was awash with verbiage. Daddy always did like to use pompous-sounding phrases when he meant something simple."

Amilou paused, then shared a memory like a peace offering. "Do you remember when he gave the commencement speech for the grammar school?"

"And little Darryl James put a tree frog under the podium." Korine could feel a smile tugging loose the stiffened muscles in her cheeks.

"Daddy was fit to be tied. He'd start a sentence like: 'All you need to aspire to in life is,' and the frog would croak. Daddy could hardly stand it when Darryl became a doctor."

Korine couldn't help but think of Doc James's expression as he stood next to Greg's grave. She caught a glimmer in Amilou's eye that might have been a tear as Amilou retook her seat. "I know how hard this is for you. You still loved Greg, didn't you?"

"Yes, I did love him. Although God alone only knows why. And no, you cannot possibly know how hard this is," Amilou said, her voice fierce. "Despite everything that man had put me through, I almost let him in when he stood on that doorstep and begged me to take him back."

Amilou disengaged her hand from Korine. "I knew about the women, Korine. And I knew everyone else knew." She picked up the discarded pencil and shaded in another portion of the roses along the back fence. "Greg was no good, Korine, so what does that make me, if I still loved him despite all that?"

Despite her best effort, Korine was not able to school her features. Amilou looked up and caught the tail end of Korine's dismay. She sagged in her chair. "You know me better than anyone else. If you have doubts, then everyone will think I did it."

"You must have hated him almost as much as you loved him." There was a sharp feeling of dismay in the pit of Korine's stomach.

"I thought I could be honest with you, Korine. It's not like I'm out front holding a press conference." This time Amilou's pencil penetrated the paper and shredded a line right through the driveway printed in the middle of the page.

She picked up the plan and tore it clear in two. Tossing it in the trash can, she pulled out another sheet of paper. "I can't begin to defend myself without the help of my friends."

Amilou began the sketch of the plan again, then threw her pencil down. "I can't do this. I can't pretend to prettify Pine Grove when I'm sick to death with worry."

Korine's reply was drowned out by the bellow of an irate voice coming over a loudspeaker in the front yard: "Get out of here right now before I arrest you for disturbing the peace."

Drawing aside the dimity curtain, Amilou and Korine peered out to see J. J. standing next to his patrol car. There were now four people outside the gate: J. J., the blue-suited woman, the fallen photographer, and Chaz.

Amilou picked up the phone and buzzed the gate open. J. J. and Chaz got in the police car and drove in.

The odd couple followed them in, which tied J. J. up for a while as he made good on his threat to arrest them for trespassing.

"Yes, I know you're just doing your job, but so am I," J. J. complained when the woman insisted that he was out of line. "Mrs. Whittier asked you not to come on her property, and you did it anyway. If you'd stayed on the sidewalk you'd've been fine."

The reporter was still arguing when J. J. rolled up his windows and drove away.

Chaz, Amilou, and Korine finished a strained lunch, all three bending over backwards to avoid talking about Greg's murder.

When the phone rang, Amilou answered it. After listening for a moment, she said, "Just a minute."

"Levy Brothers," Amilou said in response to a question on the other end of the line. After a pause, she nodded, then answered in the affirmative.

After another pause, she said, "No." Her face was alarmingly pale, but she seemed composed.

"Thank you," she said, then carefully replaced the receiver on the hook.

"That was J. J." Amilou hesitated.

The other two waited.

"Greg died around ten Thursday evening. Probably within thirty seconds after I slammed the front door in his face. And before you ask, I was alone." Amilou's composure crumbled.

"That doesn't mean anything, Amilou," Chaz said. "There are a lot of factors involved in making a case. J. J.'s a good police officer. He won't pin this on you unless you actually did it." He touched Amilou on the shoulder. "I think that means we don't have anything to worry about." Despite his words, there was a frown of concern on Chaz's face.

"But if he was killed about the same time I shut the door in his face, that also probably means he died here." Amilou crossed her arms tightly across her chest and hugged herself. "J. J. said he's releasing the body. He told me that we have to do a closed casket funeral because of 'the physical condition of the body.'"

The tears coursed down Amilou's face. Korine wrapped her arms around her friend, thrusting her earlier dismay about Amilou's revelations of her feelings for Greg into a spare storage room in her brain. Amilou clung to her, then released her abruptly. Straightening, she dashed her tears away with one hand.

Chaz said, "May I use the phone in the other room for a minute? I want to see if J. J. will fax over a copy of the autopsy report."

"Please do," Amilou responded. "I'd like to know how he died." Her voice broke.

Korine asked, "Do you want me to go with you to the funeral home?"

"Thank you." Amilou pulled away. "But I'd rather Chaz go with me. I'm more likely to cry if you're there, and I'll never get things arranged. Nicki was going to call Levy's Funeral Home about having the service on Monday. J. J. suggested that last night. Would you mind staying here and holding down the fort until we get back?"

"I'll plan on being here with you for a week or so, if you

like." Korine put every ounce of support she could into the look she gave her friend.

A strange expression passed over Amilou's face. For a minute, Korine thought she could read Amilou's mind. In the next moment, the expression was gone. Her face blank, Amilou said, "Oh no, I'm fine. Really, I'd almost rather be alone right now."

"I see," Korine said, but she didn't. Amilou was the one who had come over to stay with Korine when Charlie died. She'd said then that she hated being alone when bad things happened. Why would she want to be alone now? Was it possible that Amilou was trying to distance herself from her friends so that they wouldn't be involved if J. J. found out whatever it was that Amilou was holding back?

Chaz returned, holding a piece of paper in his hands. "Greg's throat was slit, in addition to multiple stab wounds to the . . . uh . . ." He swallowed, then looked up at Amilou apologetically.

"The 'uh' being where a scorned wife would have been sorely tempted to hit first?" Amilou was pale, her hands gripping each other as she leaned on the table.

"Uh, probably," Chaz acknowledged. "Let's go pick out the casket and talk with the minister about the service. We can talk more about this in the car. J. J.'s sending over a couple of men to go over the grounds here. I did ask him to get a search warrant, so we should have enough time to take care of the details of the funeral."

"Search warrant?" Korine asked, since Amilou seemed to be beyond speech.

"Greg was moved after he died. As Amilou pointed out, the timing is such that they feel he was killed here at The Pines."

Amilou stood and picked up her purse from the counter. Her brown eyes regarded Korine for a moment, then Amilou said, "I've changed my mind. Would you stay the night tonight?"

"Of course," Korine readily agreed.

Amilou nodded, then reached out to embrace Korine. She

hugged her, then pulled away, dashing tears from her eyes. "I don't deserve a friend like you."

"Don't be silly. Now, go on. I'll ask J. J. to wait until you get back."

"No. I don't want to be here to watch him." Amilou's brown eyes caught and held Korine's with a mute appeal. She once again hugged her friend, whispering softly, "I know I can count on you, no matter what."

That strange current returned to charge the air between them. It lingered on even after Amilou had walked out the door. Korine turned on the hot water tap. She rolled her head from shoulder to shoulder to rid herself of the tingling sensation at the base of her skull. Tucking her dismay firmly in the back of her mind, she plunged her hands deep into the hot, soapy dishwater.

CHAPTER TEN

J. J. FINISHED BOOKING IN one Louella Gerard, of *Cat Springs Inquirer* fame, along with her photographer friend about eleven o'clock. "Next time," he admonished them, "remember where public and private property leave off."

Turning to Marlene, he added, "Keep them here until bail comes through. You might want to call Juanita June and see if she'll deliver some lunch so Ms. Gerard's next column isn't about police brutality. I'm heading back over to Amilou's house."

"What about Leon?" Marlene asked.

"What about him? After this morning, he better've straightened up. I put him back on duty, off day or not. He's supposed to be out tracking down Sally Tucker's movements for the past few days."

"He hasn't called in at all."

"Did he get Claudia over to the hospital to have her checked out?"

"Yes."

"Then call and tell him to get himself in here right now." J. J. didn't quite manage to keep his tone patient.

"I've tried. He's not answering."

J. J. pursed his lips. "Well, see if you can find him. In the meanwhile, I'll take Sam and Frank over to execute this warrant." J. J. double checked to make sure he'd picked up the warrant envelope, then tucked the folder containing his notes from the day before under his arm.

"Did the lab call back with any more information for me?" he asked. Being chief of police in a small town had some definite disadvantages when investigating a murder. Lab work had to be sent out to the state crime lab, and Pine Grove always seemed to be last on the list. Still, Esther had promised.

"Yep. It's here somewhere." Marlene picked up a piece of paper and squinted at it. She pulled open a drawer and began to rummage around in it.

J. J. leaned over the counter and plucked the sheet of paper out of her hands. "Hmm. Human blood, types O positive and A positive. Bingo." J. J. smiled his satisfaction. The killer had left a calling card. "And two sets of prints on the paring knife."

Marlene held her glasses up and reached for the report. "Paring knife?"

J. J. released the paper. "Yeah, I got lucky. Evidently, the band sold them last year to get new uniforms. Everybody in town has them. What's interesting about this one, other than the blood, is that I found it out in front of Susannah's house the day after the murder."

"You think Jett and Leon missed it the first time around?"

"No. They were pretty thorough. Someone's playing games."

"Hide-and-seek?"

"What?"

"We used to sneak around and hide where 'It' had already looked."

J. J. looked at Marlene. "I suppose so. But it's a kitchen knife. The logical place to hide it, if you're thinking, is in the kitchen drawer."

Marlene squinted at the small print through her reading glasses. "This says the fingerprints were smudged. Did you do that picking it up with your handkerchief?"

"Like I've said before, Marlene, we don't do things the way they do them on the TV." J. J. sighed. "A lot of things don't add up. Either somebody's trying to frame Susannah, or she's dumber than I thought she was. For all I know, she cut her finger fixing carrot sticks for lunch and threw her knife out the window in a fit of pique and she happens to be A positive, same as Greg. Or O positive. This is just the preliminary result. They still haven't run any differentials."

J. J. checked to make sure his folder was still under his arm. "Find Leon. Tell him I said to get his sorry self on the job, and quit sniveling about his girlfriend."

On his way out, he fished a couple of quarters out of his pocket, then pushed them through the slot on the station Coke machine. He punched the button for a Coke, but nothing came out. Resisting the urge to kick the base of the machine—only because Marlene was watching him from down the hall—he headed out into the gray drizzle falling on Pine Grove.

If the weather kept up like this, Susannah Graham could thank her lucky stars that Katie Anne's garden wedding was postponed. The inside of the patrol car fogged up as soon as he got inside. The windshield looked like the inside of his brain felt.

He was looking forward to finding out where Greg was killed. One more *t* crossed off the list. J. J. wished he'd gotten that Coke. No telling what the day might bring. If it was anything like yesterday, he was going to need all the caffeine he could get.

"What do you mean, she's not home?" J. J. growled when Korine answered Amilou's door at The Pines.

"You released Greg's body. The next logical step is for Amilou to take care of the funeral." Korine stepped back and let J. J. in off the front porch.

He held his hat out the doorway behind him and shook the excess water off of it before pulling the door closed. He placed the hat carefully on the deacon's bench along the wall by the dining room. "Fair enough. I just wish *someone* was where I wanted them to be today. You couldn't happen to run to a cup of coffee, could you?"

"Better than that, we've got lunch. The church ladies stopped by."

"I'll stick to coffee," J. J. said, the country-fried steak and the funeral casserole from the night before still weighing on his mind.

"Amilou said that she thought you'd want to search her

house and that you were welcome to it. She says that since she has nothing to hide you can start as soon as you get a search warrant."

"Got it," he replied. Korine eyed with distaste the envelope that J. J. held out to her. "Amilou already gave me permission when I told her I had the warrant. Sam and Frank are outside right now. When they get done seeing what the rain's left us, they'll start inside."

Korine glanced toward the window, her movements arrested as she watched the two men outside. She turned back to J. J. "So you're really going to try and pin this on Amilou?"

"No, ma'am. I'm not going to try and pin this on anyone. I'm doing what I have to do to solve this murder. If this had happened to Charlie, I'd be searching *your* house. I don't like what needs to be done, but it's my job, and I want to do it right. I also have men out looking for Sally Tucker."

Korine didn't answer, but turned and poured a black stream from the Mr. Coffee pot. "Black, right?" She handed J. J. the mug of steaming coffee.

"Thanks." J. J. took an appreciative sip. "I hate this job sometimes, Korine. I find myself on the opposite side of an invisible line far too often. Even my friends feel guilty when they see me in uniform."

J. J. looked up to see Korine staring outside the window again, an expression of disgust on her face. She turned to him and said, "Right now, I hate your job too. But if someone had killed Charlie, I'd want that person found and punished." She looked down at her hands clasped in front of her. "I'm sorry."

"Don't worry about it. If I couldn't do my job while people were mad at me, I'd never get anything done."

"So how's Susannah holding up?" If there had been a pitcher of milk at the table, J. J. would have slid it toward Korine.

"Fine as ever." J. J. gestured toward the rain with his mug. "Although she'd never admit it, I'm sure she's just as happy not to be out there in this."

"No," Korine agreed. "Did your young officer get any useful information out of her last night?"

"Whatever Leon got out of Susannah is none of your never mind."

Korine looked at J. J. out of the corner of her eye. He'd seen that look before.

"Out with it, Korine. What are you hiding from me?" His jovial expression turned serious as soon as he saw her face take on a mulish look.

"Out with it," he repeated. If one more person today withheld information from him, he was going to lose his temper.

"Leon's been dating Claudia."

"I know that, Korine. What about it?"

"Nothing." Korine wrapped her fingers around the handle of her mug. Her hand shook slightly as she lifted the coffee to her lips.

"You wouldn't have mentioned it unless there was something. Spit it out."

Korine hesitated just long enough for J. J. to feel his temper begin to heat up his face. She took one look at him and placed the mug down on the table, carefully lining it up with the top right square in the plaid place mat. "Claudia was also seeing Greg until a few months ago. He ended their affair just before taking up with Sally."

"I found that out myself the hard way when Leon and Claudia busted up the Green Whistle."

Korine winced. "I was the one who told Leon."

"When?" J. J. barked.

"Yesterday."

"Leon knew before this morning?" J. J. knew he could look plenty mean when he wanted to. He knew what happened when you assumed things, but it had been a while since he'd been so wrong about so many things in such a short period of time. The police chief stood up. Towering over Korine, he leaned down and put his face not two inches from hers. "Korine, don't you hold anything else back from me, you hear?"

She nodded. For the first time in their association, Korine was wordless.

"Do you have anything else you'd like to share with me?"
She shook her head.

"In that case I'm going to go find Claudia and ask her a few questions that I'm sure didn't occur to Leon. Then I'm going to find my officer and put him back in gear. And if I find that you've held anything back—like another potential suspect—or twisted anything by omission, then I'm going to come and find you, too."

Korine nodded again.

"What?"

"Nothing," she said.

"Then quit bobbing your head."

"Do me a favor, J. J.?" Korine asked, recovering. "The next time you want to stand on the other side of that invisible line, could you do it a little farther back from my personal space?"

"If you don't like your personal space invaded, then don't hold things back. I know you. Claudia probably told you in confidence, and you couldn't bring yourself to tell me. If Sally's got any kind of alibi, your friend Amilou is going to look pretty good for a murder suspect. You might could think about how divided your loyalties seem to be."

He handed his cup to Korine and strode out to the hallway. He picked up his hat and jammed it on his head. "I'll do my best to sort out who did what to whom, if and when people see fit to grace me with the deep dark secrets they're bottling up inside." Throwing Korine one final glare before leaving, J. J. felt just fine about letting the door slam behind him as he went.

Korine flicked the windshield wipers on as she tried, vainly, to see past the next bank of mist rising from the wet highway. She winced when she considered what J. J. would say to her if he found out what she was doing.

For several minutes after he had stormed out, Korine alternated listening in on the officers' conversation underneath the kitchen window—hearing nothing but complaints about working in the rain—and trying to call Frieda, the county clerk's secretary, to see if she knew what Sally had been doing in the courthouse.

Finally, in desperation, she'd called Sarah Jane, Frieda's best friend as well as town gossip and mayor's wife, to see if she knew where Frieda had gone for the getaway weekend. That call took twenty minutes, but Korine prided herself that she had managed to pry the information out in record time: Frieda had gone to her mother's in Charlotte.

Frieda's mother answered the phone. After a lot of coaxing, she told Korine that Frieda was actually at her sister's in Pickles. Evidently, Frieda was resting from best friendship. That's when Korine's luck deserted her, forcing her to drive this stretch of highway between Pine Grove and Pickles. The storm that had saturated Pine Grove that morning was stalled between the two towns. The same wind and rain that made driving visibility so short had knocked out telephone service to half the county. Amilou's phone was working; Frieda's sister's was not.

Korine pulled into the empty parking lot of Grant's Feed Store when she reached the edge of town. The silence when she pulled under the front door overhang was blissful. She'd turned off the radio five miles back because she couldn't hear it, what with the rain pounding on the roof of the car. The rain fell like a blackout curtain around the overhang, cutting off the light. With one hand fishing out the piece of paper with her directions on it, she flipped on the overhead light with the other. State Street.

Korine squinted through the windshield, then back down at the note. She'd never see the street sign in this rain. She leaned over and opened her glove compartment. Chaz was always telling her that she needed to clean her car, but she never had time. She was sorry now because the contents of the glove compartment exploded like Fibber McGee's closet all over the passenger seat beside her. What made matters worse was that she didn't have a county map with her.

Grimacing from the din on the roof of the car, Korine pulled back out onto the highway. The only consolation to all this was that she wasn't standing in a tent in Susannah Graham's backyard, listening to her moan about the perfect wedding having been ruined. A street sign flashed past. Korine slowed down and put on her flashers. She crept past street after street, driving slowly at the edge of the road so that faster moving cars wouldn't hit her. Finally, her lights lit up the sign for State Street.

She turned right and began counting houses. At the fifth house on the left, she pulled in the driveway. Relieved, Korine saw that there were lights on inside the house. Someone was home. She pulled her blue and white golf umbrella out from the backseat and took a big breath. Opening the door a scant inch, she shoved the umbrella through the opening. She unfurled it, then pushed the car door open the rest of the way. The bottomless puddle she stepped into as she got out of the car rendered all this caution useless.

Shoes squelching, Korine marched up to the door. Frieda's sister, Emmie, answered quickly and let Korine in.

"As I live and breathe, it's Korine McFaile." Emmie stood on tiptoe and looked back out through the small window inset in the door. "Sarah Jane's not with you, is she?"

"No, although I talked to your mother about an hour ago and promised her that I wouldn't tell Sarah Jane where Frieda is."

"You did." The sigh of relief almost knocked Korine through the closed door at her back. "I mean: You did?"

"Emmie, don't worry. Whatever happened between Sarah Jane and Frieda, her location's safe with me." But Emmie still didn't budge and didn't invite Korine any farther than the front door. "May I see her?" Korine asked.

"Well, the truth is, she's not here, either."

"What?"

"Frieda knew Mother couldn't keep a secret, so she told her she was coming here and told Sarah Jane that she was going there."

"I'm very confused, Emmie. Wherever she is, it's pretty important that I talk with Frieda right away." Korine waited expectantly.

Emmie shifted her weight from foot to foot. "You promise not to tell Sarah Jane?"

"Cross my heart. Keeping secrets is becoming my specialty."

"She's gone on a cruise."

"Why does that have to be a secret?"

"Because Sarah Jane invited Frieda to go on this cruise with her," Emmie said, as if that explained why Frieda was sunning herself onboard ship somewhere, while Sarah Jane was sitting in the rainy weather in Pine Grove thinking that Frieda was in Charlotte.

Emmie continued, "I told Frieda, It Was Meant. I hate to speak ill of someone so sweet, but can you imagine being in a small cabin with Sarah Jane for five days?"

"Five days," Korine echoed weakly.

"I knew you'd see what I was talking about," Emmie said, misunderstanding Korine's reply. "So when only one ticket came—I don't need to tell you that Frieda's not awfully good with the Internet?"

"Reservations?" Korine took a stab in the dark.

Emmie beamed at her. "Well, she told Sarah Jane that the cruise was full."

"And went on the one ticket she'd booked?"

"Exactly. And a more deserved rest she'll never get. She was a nervous wreck that Sarah Jane would find out. So you see why you mustn't tell her where Frieda is when you get home."

Spilling the beans to Sarah Jane about her best friend's selfishness was the last thing Korine had on her mind as she drove back home through the storm. She was busy wondering how best to get a look at Frieda's logbook in the courthouse when it opened Monday morning.

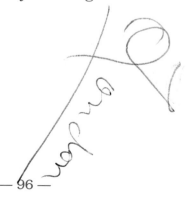

CHAPTER ELEVEN

J. J. PICKED UP THE TOP PIECE OF PAPER from his desk and ripped it in half. It was a list of suspects and their possible motives in the Whittier murder. Sally Tucker and Amilou Whittier were the only ones who really made sense if you looked at motive. But the location of the murder weapon and the body opened up other possibilities.

He swiveled his chair and looked out the window. He had never had so much trouble with a case before. *Never make friends with someone who will be suspected of murder,* he thought. *It ruins the friendship.*

A rumble in J. J.'s stomach reminded him that it ruined digestion as well. He reached into his middle desk drawer for some antacids, then picked up the ripped sheet of paper and laid the two pieces back together again.

> Sally Tucker: Jealousy? Greed?
> Susannah Graham: Jealousy?
> Dennis McFaile: Protecting Katie Anne?
> Katie Anne Graham: Protecting Susannah?
> Amilou Whittier: Money? Jealousy?

J. J. stared at Amilou's name. Just seeing a friend's name there bothered the heck out of him. When he'd opened the wrong drawer at Amilou's looking for a spoon for his coffee, he happened upon the utility drawer instead. A quick scan showed that she didn't have one of the band-sale paring knives among her collection there. To be perfectly fair, Amilou might not have bought one in the first place, or it might be in a different drawer. Or it could be down at the State Crime Lab.

His own personal favorite was Sally Tucker. J. J. didn't know her, for one thing, so he didn't have to deal with feeling guilty for arresting one of his own friends. And there was the matter of the call about Greg's life insurance.

Susannah would be his second favorite if she looked the least bit guilty. While she had pitched a fit when Greg and Amilou got married, that was twelve years back. Even though Susannah hadn't gotten married, she hadn't appeared to be pining for Greg.

Dennis and Katie Anne were dark horses indeed. No discernible reason for the two of them to have killed Greg. Yet he'd pressed Jett and Leon pretty hard about why they hadn't found the knife at Susannah's when they searched the crime scene. Both men had sworn up and down that it wasn't there when they searched. That meant that either someone in that house was playing hide-and-seek, as Marlene had suggested, or someone had planted it there for the police to find.

J. J. glared at the rain-streaked window. There were too many things he didn't like about this. Janey had been very quiet the night before when he'd asked her who she thought had done it. The moonlight from the window behind her side of the bed had obscured her expression as Janey considered his question. All she'd finally said was that she knew he would be fair and impartial. His frown deepened as he remembered their conversation that morning. She'd never really answered the question about what was bothering her.

J. J. threw the pieces of paper in the trash can and emptied his ashtray over them. Lighting up another cigarette, he picked up the phone to check on Janey. No answer. He pressed the phone back into the cradle then picked it up to call Korine to see if she'd heard from Janey. Remembering the manner in which he'd left Korine not half an hour before, he dialed Marlene instead. He wanted to know if anyone had tracked Sally down. No answer there either.

Picking himself up out of his chair, J. J. strolled down the hallway to Marlene's desk. Sure enough, sitting on the fax machine were three pieces of paper. J. J. picked them up and glanced through them. The top sheet of paper had the records from the blood bank drive last year. Susannah and Katie Anne were both O positive. J. J. scanned down the list and snorted with disgust. So were Amilou and Sally Tucker. Dennis was all alone as B positive. Greg was the only A positive one in the bunch.

J. J. wondered if it was too soon to call the lab back and ask if the tech had made the prints yet. It had been only an hour and a half. She'd promised to call. His stomach rumbled again, reminding him that he'd turned down lunch at Amilou's. He decided that if Esther hadn't called by the time he got back from lunch, then he'd call her.

"Marlene!" he yelled.

"What?" A startled Marlene popped out of the rest room. "What's wrong?"

"You're not at your desk again. What in Sam Hill is wrong with you?"

Marlene looked at him a minute. As she stared, her face turned pale, then flushed an odd shade of puce. J. J. had enough time to start reviewing the steps to CPR in his head when Marlene whirled around and dashed back through the door.

He walked over and stood outside. The strangled sounds of someone who didn't have much left inside, suffering from dry heaves, could be heard loud and clear. J. J. checked his watch. Late enough in the day that Marlene would have recovered from any drinking she had indulged in the night before. Either Marlene had developed a habit of drinking on the job in the last month or so, or he'd need a substitute dispatcher/receptionist in about seven months. Marlene's knowledge of Sally's pregnancy was explained. Doc James wouldn't disregard patient confidentiality, but comparing one woman's pregnancy to another wasn't in that league.

He left a note on Marlene's desk asking her to call him if the lab sent along any information—along with a fresh roll of Tums from his desk drawer.

The weather report on the radio was discouraging. There was small chance that they'd find any clues out of doors that would be dry enough to count. J. J. stopped by The Pines and told the two uniforms there to switch from outside to inside.

Leon still hadn't turned his radio on, or he was ignoring J. J.'s calls. Marlene probably had warned him that J. J. was on the warpath about his girlfriend.

Janey wasn't home, nor was she at Amilou's. Korine wasn't there either, which worried him. As fragile as Janey was after her spells, he didn't want Korine dragging her around on one of her wild-goose chases.

CHAPTER TWELVE

KORINE STOOD IN FRONT OF THE DOOR, barring Dennis's way into the kitchen. "You don't act like this unless something is really wrong," she said. After talking to Emmie, she had stopped by home to pack a bag before going back over to Amilou's for the night.

Looking around the hall as if he expected someone to pop out of the shadows, Dennis asked, "Is Chaz here? I need to talk to him."

Korine sighed. "He's in the kitchen. Come on in and tell us what's going on." She searched Dennis's miserable face again. "You've got your tail feathers in a spin about something. Out with it." Chaz came through the doorway from the kitchen as if on cue, giving Korine a warning look over his mug of steaming hot chocolate.

The pinched look on Dennis's face eased, but only slightly. "Chaz, can I talk to you? Alone," he added.

"Katie Anne backing out?" Chaz asked, grinning.

"No. It's not Katie Anne, it's me."

"Come along. What's this about you backing out?" Chaz's tone told Korine that he wasn't taking Dennis seriously.

"Is anything I tell you admissible in a court of law?"

"Wait." Chaz held up his hand, traffic-cop style. His expression lost its playfulness. "I've just finished picking out coffins with Amilou. Your love life sounds too complicated for me to deal with standing up. Let's go in the living room." Chaz raised one eyebrow as Korine made to follow them into the living room. "Mom, give it a rest; Dennis said 'alone.'"

Hurt, Korine said, "Don't speak to me that way."

"Even though I do still live at home," Chaz said, "I'm an adult. And if Dennis is having woman problems, then we will be able to talk about it more easily if you're not around. We are not conspiring to defraud you of something to worry over." Chaz's face took on the familiar mulish look he wore when Korine was "overmothering." She didn't mind, as long as it got him listening to his cousin.

"Fine." Korine touched Dennis's cheek as she passed by on the way to the kitchen. "But if you need me, you'll know where I am."

She went into the kitchen and pulled her African violets down from the windowsill and placed them on the counter. Next she mixed up a batch of watering solution, filling each plant's saucer. Picking the dead leaves and spent blooms from the plants, she tried to wrestle her conscience to the ground. She lost. The horrible suspicion that had taken root in her mind over Amilou's odd look that morning was more than Korine could bear to be alone with.

She took a beeline path to the darkened dining room, where she arranged herself in Charlie's old chair from the table. Sure enough, the boys were just as she had pictured them, snug in her wing chairs flanking the fireplace. From the silence between them, Dennis was still working his way up to talking about his problems. She devoutly hoped that Chaz wouldn't remember all the times he had spied on Charlie's Tuesday night poker games from this same position. With the lamps on in the living room, she could see them, but they couldn't see her.

Light danced off Dennis's wire-rimmed glasses. That, combined with the hand wringing, reminded Korine forcibly of the last time she saw a student production of Macbeth. The expression on Dennis's face made her very glad she had decided to sit in. It was a bad sign that it was taking him all this time to work up the courage to speak.

Chaz sighed. Korine wished she could pinch him to make him more receptive to his younger cousin. This was obviously more than woman trouble. Dennis was a tired and anxious young man at the end of his rope. He needed to tell Chaz who held the other end so they could untangle him.

Chaz took a sip from his chocolate and set it down carefully on a napkin. "Suppose you tell me what this is all about."

"It's Susannah."

"I thought you said you and Katie Anne broke it off?"

"We did. But it's because of Susannah—and Coach Whittier's death."

"Anything you tell me about Susannah or Katie Anne is gossip, pure and simple. I doubt very much that I'll have to pass along anything you have to say. I've got my hands full with this murder case, and while I know that Susannah is a suspect, I can't see her as the guilty party."

Dennis shifted his weight. He glanced up at Chaz, switched his gaze to the fire, then back again. Korine thought she glimpsed a note of disappointment on Dennis's face.

"Well?" Chaz prompted.

The young man slumped in his chair, looking anywhere but at Chaz. A minute ago, Dennis had been on fire to talk. Now he didn't seem to know where to begin.

"I think I need to hire you," he finally got out

"You do?"

"Yeah."

"Don't tell me: you want to confess?"

Dennis catapulted himself from the chair and walked around the room. He picked up the paperweight on Korine's desk. He hefted it in his hand, then put it down. Moving on to the bookcase he stopped.

Pulling down the family Bible, he turned and offered it to Chaz. "You might as well mark me out right now."

"What?" Chaz stared, stupidly. Dennis tossed the heavy book at him. It bounced off his knee and lay, forgotten, pages spilling open at Chaz's feet.

"I buried Greg Whittier in that flower bed. I figured it was safer than leaving him where I found him."

Korine sat, one hand covering her mouth to keep her from crying out. She was completely stunned. If Dennis had buried Greg . . .

"And where did you find him?" Chaz asked when he got his voice back.

"At the foot of Miss Amilou's front steps." Dennis leaned forward and put his head in his hands. Korine put her other hand to her face and found that she was crying.

Chaz massaged the bridge of his nose while he thought. "Mother," he called out, "you might as well come on in here. We're going to need your help on this one."

He turned back to his cousin. "Dennis, I'm not sure what to do. Representing you and Amilou at the same time would be a conflict of interest."

"But . . ."

"Please. Don't say another word," Chaz roared as Korine walked into the room. Dennis flinched from the frustration and anger in Chaz's face. "Don't you understand? Anything you say from now on, I'm duty bound to use in my client's favor."

"Then there's no problem."

"Excuse me? I think there's a problem here."

"I found him at the foot of Miss Amilou's steps, but Susannah was the one who threw the knife in the bushes I was hiding in."

"Knife? Bushes?" Chaz looked like Dennis had hit him on the *head* with the Bible, instead of on the knee.

"I followed her when she followed Greg to Amilou's house."

"What knife?" Korine asked.

Chaz held his hand up in the air again. "I'm still not sure I should let you tell me this. You can confess to Mom. Then she can tell me, and it would be hearsay."

"Hush, Chaz," Korine admonished. "Can't you see that this is to Amilou's benefit?"

Chaz rolled his eyes, but he hushed.

"Go on," Korine commanded. She felt a seed of hope stirring and didn't want it disturbed.

"Maybe Chaz is right," Dennis protested weakly.

"Go on." Korine spoke with steel in her voice.

Dennis continued: "I was going over to Katie Anne's on Thursday night. We were going to take ourselves out to dinner. Kind of an odd bachelor party, I know, but it was what we wanted. Katie Anne and Susannah were fighting, so I went back to the car to let them wind down a little. Things had just calmed down when Coach Whittier walked by. Susannah came flying out the door a minute later and followed him."

"And naturally, you pulled out and followed them? Thank goodness it was a cloudy night or the neighbors would have told J. J. about the parade that night." Chaz waved his hand weakly in the air. "I'm sorry." He quit stirring the air with his hand and began to stroke his eyebrows instead. "And then?"

"When they turned in at Miss Amilou's, I parked my car and hid in the bushes at Mrs. Potter's to see what was going on."

"It didn't occur to you to ask?" Chaz drawled.

"No." Dennis looked uncomfortable. "They'd been fighting when I drove up. I didn't want to get in the middle of it. Anyway, Coach walked up on the porch and rang the bell. Miss Amilou answered, then slammed the door. Coach walked back down the steps, then disappeared. A minute or two later, he cried out. Susannah came flying out of the driveway and tossed a knife in the bushes at me."

"Did it not occur to you to call the police?"

"If you had seen the look on Susannah's face going in, and then the absolute terror on her face going out, and had to think about marrying her daughter a few days later, you might have checked it out before calling the police."

"So you picked up the knife, then calmly went and moved a dead body?" Chaz's voice rose with disbelief.

Dennis stood up once again, this time striding to the door. "I don't know why I thought you would help. You've always treated things so, so . . ."

"Chaz, he's right. Stop being supercilious," Korine commanded.

"Come back and sit down." Chaz used his courtroom voice, which got Dennis seated in a hurry. "Who was there when you found the body?"

"Nobody. He was lying to one side of Miss Amilou's porch steps, throat slashed, very dead. Susannah had the knife.

What was I supposed to think? Miss Amilou only came out that one time that I saw."

"Again, calling the police springs to mind," Chaz said dryly. "Unfortunately, your not seeing Amilou doesn't exactly help our case. She *does* own a back door."

Dennis brightened. Korine resisted the urge to throw something at her son.

"Why did you move the body?" Korine asked.

"I didn't know what to do. For all I knew, he'd attacked Susannah, and she panicked. I didn't want Miss Amilou to have to take the blame."

"More likely Susannah would have egged him on," Korine murmured.

As long as they were tossing ideas back and forth, Korine thought she'd chance another question. "What happened between Greg and Katie Anne?"

Dennis shut his lips firmly together. "That is none of your business, Aunt Korine. She wasn't there."

"It may very well be all of our business if it led to Greg's death," Chaz reminded him. His sidelong glance at his mother told her that the importance of her question was not lost on him. "You've confessed to moving a body; the only thing worse than that is doing the killing." Chaz searched Dennis's face. "You didn't, did you? Kill him?"

"Of course not." Dennis looked from Chaz to Korine and back again. They both leaned forward toward him. Dennis's face took on the familiar pug-like look he'd inherited from his mother.

"Does what happened between Katie Anne and Greg have anything to do with why Susannah was following Greg when he went to Amilou's?" Chaz asked.

"I don't know."

"Why did you follow Susannah when she followed Greg? What did you think she was going to do?"

Dennis pressed his lips firmly together and folded his arms across his chest.

Chaz leaned back, casually kicking Korine's foot as he did so. She looked at him. He shook his head slightly. She followed his lead and leaned back in her chair. Dennis immediately relaxed his arms, but his lips still showed white against the tan of his face.

Chaz leaned forward again and, this time, reached out with one hand. "Dennis, we're not trying to put you on the spot. If there's something that Katie Anne's told you in confidence, then you don't have to tell us. However, you asked for help. You've interfered with the investigation of a serious crime. What you have to ask yourself is if this secret is germane to the crime, and whether it will help your case to share it with us."

"It doesn't have anything to do with this. I'm sure of it."

"Have you told anyone else that you moved the body?" Korine asked, winning a disapproving look from Chaz.

"What do you take me for?" Dennis answered, hands curling around the ends of the chair.

Korine was proud that neither she nor Chaz answered that question.

Chaz tented his fingertips under his chin and regarded Dennis. He tapped the tips together three times before asking another question. "Why did you feel you had to move the body? Taking the knife and leaving Greg where he was would have thrown suspicion on Amilou, not on Susannah or Katie Anne."

"I didn't want to make Miss Amilou take the blame for this. I put him where I didn't think he'd be found." Dennis looked accusingly at Korine. "Dirty Women was only supposed to do the front yard."

Korine's temper broke. "So is this my fault for agreeing to do what Susannah insisted upon? How many times have I told you to think before you act. If you're lucky, turning yourself in to J. J. will make him lean toward leniency. If you wait until he finds out on his own what you've done, then he'll lock you up and put you on trial."

Dennis turned a pleading face toward his cousin. "I promised Katie Anne I wouldn't tell anyone that Susannah was there."

Chaz shrugged his shoulders. "Then you've got a difficult

choice to make. But in my opinion, Mom's right."

"Chief Bascom would never believe this. He's never liked me."

"He doesn't dislike you. He's keeping an eye on you. Something I should have done more of recently. I thought you were grown." Korine's voice was getting shrill. She clutched the arms of the chair to keep herself from flying at her nephew.

"Mother, that's enough." The crack of Chaz's reproving voice shot across the room. "The best thing to do right now is for me to go to J. J. and tell him I have a witness who knows something important. Let me deal with him. Then if he's ready to cut a deal, I can bring Dennis in."

"Do you think he will do anything?" Dennis asked.

"Depends. If we can give him the murder weapon, then he might be more than willing to give us something."

Dennis avoided eye contact.

"Dennis?" Chaz prompted.

"I sort of lost it."

Both Chaz and Korine were struck dumb by this announcement. Korine recovered first. "What do you mean, you lost it? If you're going to pick up a murder weapon, at least put it someplace you can find it again."

"I had it in my truck. How much safer could it be? I only put it in my pocket long enough to go inside Katie Anne's," Dennis protested. "And as for picking it up in the first place, Susannah had thrown it at my head. I couldn't very well bury Greg and leave the murder weapon lying around."

"That's another thing—" Korine began.

Dennis interrupted, his face turning pink, his eyes awash with tears. "You always told me to think of others before myself. When I saw Greg lying there, and the knife had come flying out of Susannah's hand, all I could think about was all the pain that man had caused to people I care about. The way Katie Anne would feel if her mother was arrested for murder the day before her wedding. So I moved him and took the knife. I wanted to protect Katie Anne. Is that so horrible?"

Korine didn't answer. She was shaking inside because his reasoning was beginning to sound very familiar. It was an echo of the words she had been using to reconcile herself to not telling J. J. about her theory as to what lay behind Sally's courthouse visit. Protecting those you love sometimes came with a high price tag.

Chaz seized the slight pause. "Where and when did you last have the knife?"

"I had it when I knocked on the back door at Katie Anne's last night, but by the time I got into the kitchen, it was gone. Trouble was, I couldn't go look right away because Chief Bascom was talking to Susannah. I couldn't figure out how to explain poking around the yard. After he left, I had a look around. Near as I could tell in the dark, it wasn't there."

"J. J. was there? His eyes wouldn't miss something like that." Korine twisted her wedding band around her finger. "Has he mentioned anything about a weapon to you?" she asked Chaz.

"Not really, but I haven't had an opportunity to talk with him much today about specifics. We've been playing phone tag." Chaz sent Dennis an arch look, which he missed because he had sunk back into his chair and was watching the fire.

"Well, get on the phone and ask him," Korine commanded.

"Yes, ma'am, I think I will. Do you have any startling revelations you'd like to share with me to help me figure out how to best protect both my clients?"

"No," Korine lied. "Just find out who really did this."

"Oh, believe me," Chaz said, "I will. And as long as it's not one of my clients, whoever it was can rot in hell."

Korine watched her son stride angrily out of the room and prayed that her seed of hope wouldn't wither.

CHAPTER THIRTEEN

BY THE TIME KORINE PACKED her bag and got back to The Pines, Amilou's house was full of well-wishers. Once again cornered by a neighbor, Amilou turned away from Korine's raised eyebrow. Evidently, she didn't want any help.

Korine twitched the sheer drape back and watched the rain overwhelm the gutters. A curtain of water cascaded down, smashing Amilou's prize peonies to the ground. Her garden looked like a waterlogged Monet. Pretty, if you liked the washed-out, beaten-up look.

Down by the gate a black form stood under an umbrella. A break in the rain allowed Korine a better look at the bedraggled figure. Katie Anne Graham. Korine frowned. What was she doing out there staring at the house? Didn't the girl have the sense God gave a cat to come in out of the rain?

Korine dropped the curtain and made her way through the crowd to Amilou. She might have waved Korine away earlier, but now Amilou had her spine pressed up against the wall. Mary Faye Crosley was usually a well-intentioned woman. But at that moment, Amilou was doing more comforting than being comforted.

"I cannot believe this happened in our town," Mary Faye said, a continuous stream of tears flooding her face. The whole effect was similar to the view outside the window, Korine thought uncharitably. Soggy and smeared. Amilou and Korine exchanged a look that almost made up for the cold reception that Korine had gotten earlier.

She'd arrived over an hour ago. Amilou had been avoiding her ever since, almost as if she regretted her earlier promise to entrust Korine with her problems. Korine handed Mary Faye a tissue and helped her to wipe away the traces of mascara and eye shadow damage. "There. Good as new," she lied.

"I don't know how you can be so calm. Who knows who will be next?"

Amilou replied, "We don't have a serial killer on our hands here."

"I don't think you have a thing to worry about, Mary Faye." Janey's lilting voice came from behind Korine.

Mary Faye suddenly noticed someone she had to talk to across the room. Janey watched her go, her face more impassive than usual. A few years before, Mary Faye had touted Janey as the best maid she'd ever had. Now, she ignored her whenever she could.

"When did you sneak in?" Amilou asked, breaking the silence.

"We got caught in the downpour finishing up at Susannah's, so I took the time to wash up at home before coming over. Just got here."

"We?"

"Nicki and Janey finished up for us." Korine answered for Janey.

"I wondered what we were going to do about her yard. Did J. J. let you cover up the . . ." Amilou's eyes shifted, her gaze landing on the group of church ladies that Mary Faye had joined on the far side of the dining room table.

"We just did the front," Janey answered. Her eyes focused intently upon Amilou's face. "Do you need anything done in particular around here?"

Korine watched Amilou tear her attention away from the gossiping women. Every now and again one of them would look at the three friends, then turn away and whisper intently. "Yes, could you get all these people out of here?" Amilou shrugged at Janey's assessing look. "They're all looking at me the same way that you are: 'Did she? Didn't she?' True, we were almost divorced, but I still loved the man Greg was when I married him."

Janey looked at the nearest group of people. As she did, Sylvester, that perennial campaigner, turned. He gave Janey an all-over stare, not bothering to disguise what was on his mind. Korine could almost feel the hate spewing from his narrowed eyes. When he saw the trio of them returning his regard, he swiveled back around so fast that his toupee almost came off. "I know what you're talking about," was all Janey said.

Amilou's face inflamed. "I'm sorry. You do know how it feels. It's creepy, knowing what people think of you."

"That's because you've always been liked," Janey said matter-of-factly.

"Now, would you look at that," Korine said, desperate to change the subject. She pointed out the window at a small break in the clouds. "The weather's breaking. Which means you're going to have more visitors in about an hour. I'll second Janey's offer of help."

"Mary Faye is supposedly in charge of the tables, but she hasn't stopped crying long enough to look at them. Perhaps you could gently take that over?"

"We'd be happy to." Janey laid a hand on Amilou's arm. "They'll find something else to talk about soon enough. You'll want to stay calm so their attention will move on to the next crisis instead of dwelling on this one." Janey pushed Amilou toward her guests. "Go on. Be gracious. They'll leave soon enough."

Amilou and Korine both stared at the door to the kitchen as it swung shut behind Janey. The front doorbell rang, and someone opened it to admit a bevy of visitors. Korine put her arm around Amilou and squeezed. "I know all you want to do is run away as fast as you can, but Janey's right. Don't let these biddies have that satisfaction."

"Why shouldn't I run away? You did." Amilou's voice was sharp. Forcing a smile onto her face, she turned away and descended on Sylvester.

Rebuffed, Korine returned to the kitchen. Her stomach still wrenched with dismay over Amilou's behavior. Or was it her own behavior? A small voice reverberated deep inside her. Korine needed to talk to Amilou and find out what was really going on. She could leap to as many conclusions as she wanted, but it was doing neither of them any good at all.

"Can you hand it to me?" Janey's question cut through the fog in Korine's mind.

"I'm sorry, what do you need?"

"I need to cut up some more carrots. I can't reach the knife drawer."

"Sure," Korine said, sliding the drawer open. Reaching in, she pulled out a knife at random and handed it to Janey.

"Amilou has one of those band knives, doesn't she? That one will work better."

Korine bent her head over the drawer and looked. Pushing the top layer aside, she looked again. Shoving the drawer back in with her hip, she said, "That one'll have to do. It's the only suitable chopping knife in there."

"She had one, didn't she?"

The persistence of Janey's questions finally got through to her. "What are you doing?" Korine asked, turning to stare at Janey.

"A band-sale knife was used as the murder weapon."

Korine put a hand onto the counter to support herself. "You're checking up on Amilou for J. J.?" Her voice was hoarse. It was difficult to keep herself from blurting out her dismay that J. J. had found the knife which Dennis had dropped.

"Not for J. J., for Amilou. J. J.'s already searched the house, so he'll know if Amilou is missing one or not. But I won't ask him what he found." Janey took a step closer to Korine and lowered her voice. "Even with what I said earlier, I've reconsidered. I've been watching Amilou. She *is* hiding something, but I don't believe it's murder."

Korine didn't trust herself to answer. She couldn't blame Janey any longer for thinking that Amilou might be capable of killing her husband. After all, Korine had been thinking just that all the way to Pickles and back again. Greg had died here in Amilou's garden. Blast Chaz for pointing out that Amilou could have gone out the back door as easily as the front.

Despite her earlier confession of the need to talk to Korine, Amilou was hiding something from her. What else did she have to hide? Korine picked up a tray and backed through the swinging door to the hallway.

Katie Anne must have decided that she was wet enough. She came through the front door as Korine went into the dining room.

"Why hello, bride-to-be," the Reverend Edward Richardson said as he held the door for Katie Anne.

Katie Anne walked past the minister as if he weren't there, looking left and right. Several people spoke to her, but she didn't stop. Korine put the platter down and watched, frowning, as Katie Anne searched the crowd.

The doorbell rang again, and someone Korine didn't know opened the door to admit Susannah.

"I know Katie Anne's here. Her car's outside. I need to speak to her." Susannah's voice squeaked like it needed oiling after the rain.

Katie Anne's head whipped around. She ducked into the kitchen just as Susannah came into the dining room. Korine stepped forward and intercepted Susannah before she could go after her daughter. She had no idea what the Graham women were doing here, but the last thing any of them needed was a scene. Knowing what she knew about Susannah's being on the spot for Greg's death made it imperative to get her out of the spotlight.

"It's good of you to come and offer Amilou your condolences," Korine said, putting a staying hand on Susannah's arm.

"That hussy's not getting anything from me," Susannah hissed. "Let go of me and let me have my baby back."

"Katie Anne is here, but she showed up of her own accord; no one is keeping her captive."

"You've been turning her against me."

"You've been doing fine all on your own," Korine muttered under her breath, opening the swinging door to the butler's pantry between the dining room and the kitchen. While Korine had never had the depth of feeling for The Pines that Amilou did, the grandeur of the place did afford some niceties that came in handy. The small room was lined with shelves covered with glass-fronted cabinets. It was also off the beaten path for visitors, who would use the door that led directly into the kitchen.

"What is going on?" Korine asked. "Dennis called last night, something about Katie Anne running away. Did he find her, and what happened?" She chose not to confront Susannah, trusting Chaz to take care of Dennis his way.

"I wouldn't know. I haven't seen her since your nephew drove her out of my house last night. I had to hear it from Carlotta Fuller next door to me that my own daughter was arrested last night. I was on my way to the jailhouse when I saw Katie Anne's car, here of all places."

"Wait, back up. Katie Anne was arrested last night?" Dennis hadn't mentioned this part.

"Yes, and I have to find my baby and find out what's going on."

"She's in here," Korine said. She pushed open the kitchen door. Susannah bolted through and stopped short at the sight of Katie Anne sitting at the table with Amilou and Janey.

"I keep it right there. Where has that knife gotten to?" Amilou said as she looked up at Janey, her brow wrinkled with confusion. It was inevitable that she also caught sight of Susannah and Korine standing behind Janey. Katie Anne's face lost what little color it had as her head swung around to follow Amilou's stare. Janey got up and retreated to the sink.

Ever since Korine could remember, the kitchen table was where life happened. News was shared, woes were comforted, and blessings were bestowed there. It was a fitting place for these three women to resolve their problems. That was, if they could get to that point without coming to blows.

"I needed to talk with you," Katie Anne got out. "I know . . ." Her voice failed her.

Amilou flushed. Susannah started forward suddenly and Katie Anne flinched. Janey came over and stood next to Korine. "Do you think I should call J. J.?" she whispered in Korine's ear.

"Did you know that Katie Anne was arrested last night?" Korine hissed at Janey.

"What?!" Janey blurted out. "Not that sweet girl?"

"I guess not." Korine said, moving toward the table. Janey put her arm out and grasped Korine's wrist.

"You've got to let them sort this out," Janey said in a low, even voice. All of Korine's nerve endings were jumping. Janey's skin was cool and dry where her fingers encircled Korine's wrist. Korine slowly turned her hand over and grasped Janey's slim fingers in return.

Janey was right. This was between Katie Anne and her mother and Amilou. Whatever had happened last night had nothing to do with Greg Whittier. Korine held her breath at the girl's next words.

Katie Anne looked up at Amilou and asked, "Did you love your husband?"

Before Amilou could answer, Susannah stepped forward. "That hardly matters, he left her."

Katie Anne gave her mother a violently hateful glance, then dismissed her, turning her attention back to Amilou. "Did you love him still?" the girl pressed. "Did he ever love you? He told me that he loved me."

"I'm sorry," Amilou said. "He had a gift for saying that and making everyone believe that he meant it for her ears alone. And yes, despite everything he put me through, God help me, I still loved him. Even though I sent him away that last night, I still loved him." Amilou began to rock back and forth, and a soft keening issued from behind the shaking hands she'd used to cover her face.

"Call J. J. This is already beyond what you and I can handle." Korine broke away from Janey's hold and brushed past an immobile Susannah. Leaning over, she put her arms around Amilou. The door to the dining room opened and closed. Janey was away.

Amilou's shoulders felt like set cement, unable to bow, even after all the pressure she'd been under the last few days. Katie Anne reached out and touched Amilou's arm gently. "Did you kill him?"

Amilou pushed Korine away and stood up. "Get out of my house! So my knife is missing. Your mother's is too. You said that Greg said he loved you. Did you kill him when he decided that he liked Sally better than he liked you?"

"He never touched you!" Susannah pulled her daughter around to face her.

"He bothered *all* the girls, Mother. What makes you think he wouldn't touch me?" Korine got the feeling that Katie Anne was baiting Susannah, daring her to answer.

Susannah stood before her daughter, head bowed, fists clenching and unclenching. A single tear inched out of the corner of her eye and rolled down her powdered cheek. Rounding on Amilou, Susannah hissed, "You never deserved him."

"Get her out of my house," Amilou begged Korine. "I won't be responsible for what I'll do to her if you don't."

Reluctantly, Korine turned to try and soothe Susannah. Korine slipped and fell as she ducked a blow from Susannah's flashing hand.

"He wasn't your husband any longer," Susannah said. "You couldn't bear it that he had chosen someone other than yourself, could you?"

"Greg was coming home. If I'd taken him back, he wouldn't be dead now."

"You're lying. Greg told me he would never come back to you no matter how much you begged. You couldn't take it, so you killed him. Then you buried him at my house to make it seem like I killed him."

Korine had scrambled out of the way. Using the counter edge, she hauled herself back up. A tearful Katie Anne cowered in her chair, looking from one angry woman to the other.

What on earth was taking J. J. so long?

CHAPTER FOURTEEN

J. J. PICKED UP THE PHONE on the third ring. "What?" he barked.

Janey's sweet voice said, "Can you come over to Amilou's?"

"Honey, I'll be over shortly to talk to Amilou. Right now, I'm in the midst of yelling at Leon for withholding evidence."

Leon slid down another inch in his seat at the look J. J. threw him.

"Amilou and Susannah are about to kill each other over here. Katie Anne came in here with some garbled story about her mother missing her knife too. I think she must have been really thrown when you arrested her last night."

"I didn't arrest her. All those women are unhinged."

J. J. fell silent, eyeing the pair of sorry-looking people sitting on the opposite side of his desk. It was not one of his better days, having run through one disaster after another. Leon's disappearing trick had not helped. J. J. knew full well that he should have been over to talk to all three of those women this morning, but he hadn't been able to get to it.

"I'll be right there." J. J. slammed down the phone and glared at the officer and his girlfriend seated across the desk from him. "Leon, get yourself in gear. That was Janey. Evidently, *two* of our suspects are missing their kitchen knives. That leaves both Susannah and Amilou with means as well as motive. My wife had to call in this information because a certain paid member of my police force has been playing with his personal life rather than coming in to work."

"We going to make an arrest?" Leon asked, looking about as relieved as a subordinate could look and still be in a heap of trouble.

J. J. didn't answer the question, just gave Leon a cold, hard stare. Better to let him stew. "Claudia, you run on home. I'll call you later to verify everything you've finally told me. The next time you withhold evidence, I'm going to slap you both in jail. Do you hear what I'm saying?"

"Yes, sir," both Leon and Claudia said in unison.

"Sally Tucker'd better turn up soon. Although, with the way things are going, she'll be missing her kitchen knife too. C'mon with me for now. This may require two police officers." J. J. picked up his hat and used it to shoo the two young people out of his office.

He stopped by Marlene's desk to let her know he was leaving. No surprise, she was away from her desk. He reached over to get the pad of paper on her desk and ripped the top page off. He glanced at it and crammed it into his pocket. If Chaz's call was so urgent, he could show up in person. J. J. scribbled a note to Marlene telling her where he'd be, then tossed the pad back on her desk.

There was a hint of sunshine when he and Leon hit the parking lot. Despite the fact that Amilou's knife was missing, Susannah's was too. J. J. felt more optimistic than he had since Friday morning. Perhaps the break he'd been hoping for was coming through. The only cloud left in his day was the fact that another cabin was broken into that afternoon. And the fact that Sally Tucker had eluded them again, leaving Jett in her dust as she skidded out of the Wal-Mart parking lot not an hour ago.

J. J. didn't slow down, even when his foot slid into a leftover mud puddle as he got to the car. He tried not to speed going over to The Pines, but he couldn't help himself. He just wanted to get his hands on someone who would actually tell him something he didn't already know.

Leon was right behind him when he turned in the side street to The Pines. Amilou's house was packed with folks come for a bite of Saturday night supper and chatter about the murder. J. J. parked around back so as not to give them more to talk about. Not waiting for Leon to get out of his car, he mounted the steps to the kitchen door.

Janey opened it and pulled him in. "You'd better get in here quick. Susannah and Amilou are about to kill each other. Something is really wrong with Katie Anne."

"Wait just a minute. Are you telling me one of them has confessed?"

Janey tugged on J. J.'s arm. "Nooo." His wife's eyebrows knit themselves together as she frowned at him. "Would you get in there? Keep them from getting hurt now, figure out who to arrest later."

J. J. relented and followed Janey into the kitchen. She had not underestimated the situation. Amilou and Susannah stood inches from each other, hands on hips, words flying fast and furious. The gist of the hissing and spitting was, "You did it."

He was not encouraged to see that both of them seemed to believe what they were saying. He waded in past Katie Anne, cowering in a chair. Korine, who had a nasty looking black eye coming up, backed out of his way as soon as she saw him coming. J. J. lowered a restraining hand onto each of the women's shoulders.

"Sit down!" he yelled, when neither of them responded. He shoved Susannah around the table into one of the pine chairs and then reached over and gathered a handful of Amilou's shirt in his hand as she tried to follow Susannah.

Amilou rounded on him. Her open palm hit his cheek with a loud crack. Leon burst through the door and cuffed Amilou before J. J. could say "boo."

"You idiot, take these off me!"

"You assaulted a police officer," Leon explained.

"Leon, take them off. She didn't hurt me."

"But, sir," Leon protested. His young face was genuinely bewildered.

"Go ahead and take them off. We're not arresting Amilou right now." J. J. turned his attention to Amilou. "I'm letting it slide. This time."

Amilou didn't look as grateful as she ought to.

"Now, everybody, sit down," J. J. said.

"It's my house," Amilou argued.

"I don't care! Put it down right there," he roared, finally out of patience. She sat.

J. J. towered over the three seated at the table. He let his regard come to rest briefly on a weeping Katie Anne, then Susannah, then at last, Amilou. Of the women, only Amilou met his eyes squarely. From the mulish look on her face, it was probably a measure of how angry she was with him. Susannah and her daughter both tucked their faces into a mess of tissues from the box that Janey had passed around.

"Leon, go get those people out of here," J. J. said. The curious face of Mary Faye and a few of her cronies peered around the corner. They disappeared as Leon moved in their direction. He continued on through the swinging door to the dining room, where he could be heard trying not to explain too much to Mary Faye.

"What's all this about?" J. J. asked.

A wail emerged from behind Katie Anne's Kleenex.

J. J. grabbed a chair. Turning it around, he straddled it and laid his arms across the back. Picking the line of least defense, he asked his first question: "Okay, Katie Anne, I understand that you came over here in a state. Suppose you tell me what you've found out."

The only answer was muffled sobbing.

"She doesn't know what she's talking about. The strain—"

"Susannah, when I want a contribution from you, I'll ask for one. Until then, keep it quiet."

J. J. turned back to Katie Anne. "Sweetheart, most brides have enough to contend with, just getting to the altar. Having a dead man turn up in your yard isn't on the usual fare."

Susannah moved. J. J. fixed her with his sternest look. She subsided. He continued, his voice low and even. "I need to ask you some hard questions."

Katie Anne emerged from behind the Kleenex, looking like a bloodshot blonde raccoon. "She didn't kill him."

"She?"

"Mother . . ." Katie Anne dove for the tissues again.

Susannah said, "Honey, you don't have to do this!"

"Susannah, I warned you once. I'm not doing it again."

"I didn't do anything. She did it." Susannah collapsed, sobbing in her daughter's arms, one trembling hand outstretched, pointing at Amilou.

"Leon!" J. J. roared.

Leon came skittering through the swinging door from the dining room. "Sir?"

"Make sure this woman doesn't move from that chair. Katie Anne, you come with me," J. J. said, standing. He'd had about as much hysterics as he could stand.

Katie Anne followed his lead, holding herself up with an obvious effort.

"I'll need to talk with all of you eventually. Leon, stay here and make 'em behave." J. J. turned back to Amilou. "Is there a room that I can use to talk with Katie Anne in private?"

"Katie Anne needs a lawyer to talk to you," Susannah choked out through her tears, drowning out Amilou's reply.

J. J. leaned over Susannah and said, "The next time you open your mouth, I'm going to let Leon, here, cuff you and run you in for obstruction of justice. Am I making myself clear to you yet?" To Katie Anne he said, "Do you want a lawyer? You don't have to talk to me without one, you know."

"Are you going to arrest me again? I haven't done anything wrong," Katie Anne said, but her eyes filled again with tears.

J. J. didn't know what to say to her. Instead he turned to Amilou. "Which room did you say?" he asked.

"The front room upstairs," Amilou replied. Korine stood next to her friend, ready to do battle on her behalf, J. J. supposed.

As Katie Anne left the room with J. J., she walked up the stairs without looking back at her mother. Janey stepped in and folded a now-silent Susannah into her arms. J. J. stalked up the steps behind Katie Anne, heartily wishing that Greg Whittier had never come back to Pine Grove.

"You sure you're okay to talk?" J. J. softened his voice.

Katie Anne looked all to pieces, as she would be with all she'd been through the last few days. The poor girl needed a father's advice right now, something she'd gone without for a long time. On the other hand, it was very possible that she knew who was guilty and that she was withholding evidence. That thought strengthened J. J.'s determination to find out just what was causing Katie Anne's behavior.

"I'll be fine. I haven't done anything wrong."

"I'm sure you haven't. I may need to use things that you say in my investigation. I'm going to turn this tape recorder on. Is that okay with you?"

Katie Anne regarded the small black machine. Without meeting J. J.'s searching gaze, she nodded.

"Out loud, honey. For the tape."

"Yes, it's okay." Katie Anne's voice was soft, but J. J. thought the tape had gotten it.

"Where were you Thursday night?"

"At home."

"And who was there with you?"

"Mother. Later in the evening Dennis stopped by."

"I see." J. J. couldn't be sure, but he detected a hesitation in her answer.

"So you never left the house?"

"No." The answer was delivered in a hoarse whisper. Her red-rimmed eyes flicked up to meet his searching gaze, then slid away.

J. J.'s hunch was right. Katie Anne knew something she hadn't shared with him yet. "And your mother?"

Another hesitation, this time a few heartbeats long. "She took a short walk, but it was early."

"And she was home when Dennis stopped by?"

"Oh, yes. She was long gone to bed by the time he stopped in." Relief softened her voice.

"Miss Graham, I'm going to ask you again if you left the house that night."

Frightened blue eyes peered at him from behind smeared mascara. "No, I didn't leave the house. I swear it."

J. J. took his time over the next question, giving Katie Anne time to imagine that he knew more than he did. Her blue eyes grew even wider. She stared at J. J. as if she were trying to read his mind.

"When your mother left, was it because of the fight you two were having concerning Greg Whittier?"

It was like watching a late summer storm come up. Katie Anne's eyes filled with tears. A split second later, she looked like she would drown in the tears flowing down her face. "I don't know," she wailed. A babble of unintelligible words poured from her lips, keeping pace with her heaving sobs.

"Katie Anne, take some deep breaths." J. J. wasn't sure what to do. Holding her as he held Janey during one of her spells wasn't an option. Even if it was a well-intentioned gesture, Lord only knew what Sylvester would do with that in his campaign for sheriff. J. J. crossed over to the door and called downstairs for his wife. He needed to calm Katie Anne down enough to find out what she thought she knew.

When he'd talked to her the day before, she'd lied when he asked her if she knew anyone who would want to harm Greg. He didn't know why he'd let this slide. Anyone with sense would know that Greg was bound to bring tension into this family. He'd been too much a part of this pair of women's lives to slip into a pre-wedding atmosphere without causing ripples.

Janey ran up the steps. "What is it?" Her soft brown eyes were filled with worry.

"Katie Anne's lost control. I need help calming her down. It may be that she knows something about this case. But it might just be what's happened with the wedding. I need a female officer to calm her down. Can I deputize you?"

Janey's quick smile told J. J. that he had done the right thing. She edged past him into the room. Putting one hand out, she barred his way through the door. "Give me a minute."

Not one, but five minutes later, the door opened, and a now-silent and scrub-faced Katie Anne sat quietly on her chair. Janey took the chair by the door after closing it behind J. J.

"Are you ready to continue?"

"Yes."

Whatever Janey had said to the girl, it wrought a miracle. Her eyes were clear. Her hands lay calm on top of the faded blue of her jeans.

"Suppose you tell me about what happened that night."

"Mother and I were fighting because she let Greg Whittier stay with us. I wasn't sure why he was there." Katie Anne paused and looked to Janey as if for a cue. Janey nodded encouragement but didn't speak.

"I was afraid . . ." A sigh escaped Katie Anne. When she continued, her voice was stronger than it had been since they entered the room. "I was afraid that Mother invited him home for the wedding. As it turned out, I was half right."

J. J. regarded the girl in front of him. She seemed to assume that she'd told her whole story. There was a leap there that he couldn't follow. He thought over the curious choice of wording. Why would Susannah have invited Greg "home" for the wedding? Unless Katie Anne thought that Greg was going to get back together again with her mother.

As if reading his mind, Katie Anne paled. The three sat quietly for a moment, even the tape winding into stillness from the quiet.

J. J. shifted his weight. "So Susannah invited Greg home for your wedding. Did she think you'd allow that?"

"I don't think she would have cared what I thought if she could get him back again."

Janey sat forward. "You said earlier that Greg bothered *all* the girls. Honey, did he try anything with you while he was here this time?"

Katie Anne shook her head wordlessly. Her eyes looked suspiciously moist. J. J. was not about to make her repeat that answer out loud for the tape, for fear of starting up the crying again, so he made a note on his pad and continued.

"Did you ever have any sort of relationship with Greg other than student/teacher?" J. J. saw her hesitate before nodding her head. His heart sank. If Greg were still alive, he'd line up for a chance to hit him. Katie Anne had a child's need for a father. What a blow it must have been to have Greg bother her.

J. J.'s eyes narrowed as he took in the signs of grief that Katie Anne displayed. A nasty thought occurred to him. Was it possible that Katie Anne had welcomed Greg's attentions?

"Did Greg come to your house for you, or for your mother?"

Katie Anne's blue eyes shone with sorrow as she slowly nodded her head, then shook it. "I just don't know."

J. J. sat and watched Katie Anne. There was a world of hurt in that last statement. It was time to press a little harder. "I'm going to talk with Susannah next, you know."

"All I know is that he showed up Wednesday around dinnertime, asking to stay with us. He did say that Sally had turned out to be a great disappointment to him."

J. J. shifted to a slightly different tact. "What time did Dennis stop by on Thursday night?"

This question was rewarded with the hunching together of Katie Anne's shoulders. She maintained eye contact, however. Whatever it was that Katie Anne was hiding, it wasn't about Dennis.

"Around eleven."

"That's kind of late to come calling."

"He often came by after work. You know he worked two jobs to buy me my engagement ring."

J. J.'s glance fell to her left hand. And she'd just thrown it away. Cold little thing. One of his eyebrows inched upward in spite of himself.

"I talked with his employer earlier. He wasn't working that night, Katie Anne. You do know that, don't you?"

The small table next to Katie Anne's chair crashed to the floor as she jumped up. "What are you saying?"

"Are you sure you didn't leave the house? Or did you meet Dennis here at The Pines?"

"No! I've told you twice. I was at home. Mother came in and went right to bed around nine. Dennis came around eleven. I was making rice bags. I'd be happy to show them to you."

Katie Anne's restless pacing took her around the room. She begged Janey for corroboration. "You know how long it takes to make those things? I was there for hours tying ribbon."

"Were either Susannah or Dennis behaving strangely?"

Katie Anne stopped in her tracks as if struck. She collapsed into the chair and folded her arms across her chest. "I want a lawyer," were the last words J. J. got out of her.

After five minutes of trying different questions with no reply, J. J. gave up. "Janey, can you take Katie Anne downstairs? Ask Leon to bring Susannah up here, and don't let the two of them talk. I want to find out what these two ladies are hiding. If one of them won't talk, the other will."

CHAPTER FIFTEEN

J. J. BARELY FINISHED putting another tape in his machine before Susannah's outraged voice ricocheted up the stairs. The yelling came closer, so he figured Leon was handling things just fine on his own.

"Let go of my arm, young man!" Susannah burst into the room in a whirl of accusation. "What did you do to my daughter? Why can't I see her? Who do you think you are?"

"Have a seat," was all J. J. gave her back.

"I will not say a word until I've seen my baby."

"Well then, we'll be here a while, because you won't be leaving this room until you've answered a few questions. Or would you rather go down to the jail and sit a spell until I'm ready for you again? Your choice."

Susannah crossed her legs and pouted. "You can't treat us this way."

"On the contrary, I've been extraordinarily patient. I'm investigating the murder of a man last seen in your home. I've tried being nice, but I'm not getting the information that I need."

Susannah graced J. J. with a look of barely suppressed fury, then pressed her lips together while folding her arms across her chest. She didn't seem to understand that cooperation was the password here.

"Your daughter's made some interesting statements. I don't want the two of you getting together until I've heard your version."

"Well, I never!"

"Cut it out. You're too mature a woman for that old Southern Belle act."

"What did Katie Anne tell you?" Susannah asked suspiciously. When J. J. didn't answer, she continued, "Katie Anne's been so unlike herself. I don't know if she'll ever recover from losing Dennis."

J. J. was sick to death of listening to Susannah's whiny voice. Tossing tact to the wind he asked, "Is it recovering from losing Dennis, or recovering from losing Greg?"

Susannah went white. Drawing herself up, she said, "I've told you before that Katie Anne was off-limits to Greg, and he knew it."

"Evidently that didn't stop him," J. J. said flatly.

Susannah's face powder stood out, etching the lines around her nose and mouth as if she had been carved from frosted glass. She stood up and began to walk over to the door.

"Sit down and listen up, Susannah." J. J. towered over the woman as Leon blocked the door. "You're in a heap of trouble here. Settle down. Understood?"

Leon herded her back into the chair again.

"Now, suppose you tell me how and why Greg Whittier came to be staying at your house."

"He came to me." Susannah's breathing was still rapid, but J. J. thought he saw a little calm creep into her eyes.

He held his own temper in check and asked, "Why did Greg need someone to come to?"

"Sally made him leave The Depot. Greg said that she had been acting strange all day Wednesday. They had a little tiff, and she left to cool off. When she got back, she was angrier than ever. She actually threw his suitcase out on the sidewalk."

"So why did he pick you?"

"We've always been special friends."

"I see. So when he got into trouble, he turned first to you?"

Far from the reaction he expected, Susannah simpered and said, "Of course. Greg knew we'd always take him in."

"Did you know about Katie Anne's relationship with Greg?"

Susannah's eyes narrowed. "Leave her out of this. She had nothing to do with his death." Her expression altered subtly.

J. J. was surprised by the look Susannah directed at him. *Why would she pity him?* He threw another question at her: "And how do you know that? Where were you when Greg died?" J. J. sank back into his chair.

"When did he die?" Susannah asked, the expression in her eyes demurely shaded by her lashes as she considered the patterned rug on the floor at her feet.

"You were out walking about the time Greg died."

Susannah raised her eyes to meet J. J.'s. "Oh, I didn't really walk. Katie Anne and I had one of those pre-wedding jitters spats. I just went outside to cool off for a time. There's a nice bench around back by the wellhouse."

"And you stayed there?"

"Of course."

"And do you remember when Dennis stopped by?"

"J. J., honey, I was exhausted. I went to bed early so I could be up the next day to supervise the landscapers. Dennis often stopped by after work; he may have been there Thursday evening."

"Dennis didn't work that night. Why do you suppose he got there so late? Could he have been out killing Greg so that Katie Anne wouldn't be troubled by him on her wedding day?"

Susannah's brows slowly rose. "Dennis didn't work Thursday night? I wonder where he was." She held J. J.'s gaze, unblinking.

He wondered how she could point so callously to her daughter's intended. Was that just a ploy to keep him away from Katie Anne, or was Dennis somehow involved? Running with it, he asked, "Would Dennis do anything Katie Anne asked him to do?"

Susannah was out of the chair, her hands like bobcat claws reaching for his face before J. J. finished the question. He caught her wrist and forced her back. Leon took hold of Susannah's shoulders and held her while J. J. got out of range.

She pulled against the hold Leon maintained on her arms. For the first time that J. J. had ever seen, there was no trace of the coquette left in her eyes. "I've told you over and over again," she hissed. "Katie Anne never had anything to do with Greg's death."

"You'd better go ahead and take her down to the station," J. J. said wearily.

"You didn't arrest Amilou!"

"No, but she stopped when I asked her to the first time. I'm not sure that you will."

Despite the fact that Amilou had the best motive—barring what he hadn't been able to find out about Sally Tucker—something very odd was going on with Katie Anne and Susannah. Once he got these two buttoned down, he could send Leon back out after Sally. J. J. still favored her. After all, why run away from the police if you hadn't done anything wrong?

He followed Leon downstairs and collected Katie Anne from Janey. As soon as they got back to the station, he was going to send Leon out with the instructions not to count on going off duty until he found that blasted Sally Tucker and brought her in.

"Chief, this came in while you were gone," read the sticky note on top of the report from the pathologist's office. He picked it up from his desk and scanned it quickly, then sat down heavily at his desk. Leon ushered Katie Anne into the straight-backed chair on the other side. The ride in the cruiser over to the police station from Amilou's seemed to have steadied her nerves.

Her mother, on the other hand, was still squawking down the hall in the jail cell. Susannah had fought Leon all the way out the door, earning herself some time behind the barred door at the end of the hall.

J. J. pressed the button on his intercom. "Marlene, would you go close the door to the jail, please. Mrs. Graham is upsetting my witness."

Marlene's footsteps tapped past the open door. The sound of the heavy door closing caused Katie Anne to shiver.

"Now, suppose you tell me again what happened Thursday

night," J. J. said, propping himself on the front corner of the desk close to Katie Anne.

"I've told you."

"So tell me about Greg. When did you begin your relationship with him?"

"I beg your pardon?"

"Your relationship with Greg Whittier. When did it begin?"

Katie Anne stared at him a moment, then shook her head slightly.

"I guess you could say that I had an ongoing relationship with Greg Whittier."

J. J. felt sick. Greg must have started on the girl when he was dating Susannah. He picked up the lab report and scanned it again. Looking back up at Katie Anne, he let his features harden. Personal sympathy aside, he had to get some information from this girl. Much as he hated to look at it in that light, she had a hell of a motive.

"What is it?" Katie Anne asked suspiciously.

"The lab report from the state crime lab."

The girl froze. Bewildered blue eyes looked up at J. J. through the fringe of her lashes, nearly melting his heart.

Waiting a minute, he held her gaze. Then he said, "I'm going to need to fingerprint you to see if you match the second set. I sent down a few sets I'd already collected. They found a match with one of them."

Those blue eyes got even wider. J. J. handed her the paper. Breaking eye contact with an effort, Katie Anne bent her head and began to read. She traced down the page with the broken nail at the tip of her index finger. When she came to the line identifying the owner of the matching prints, she let go of the paper as if it had caught fire.

"Dennis didn't do this!"

"You want to tell me who did?"

"I don't know!" The wail sounded genuine.

"Then tell me how Dennis's prints got on the murder weapon."

"He could have picked up the knife anywhere. He's in and out of lots of people's houses. His Aunt Korine's, Miss

Amilou's—"

"Yours."

One hand to her left temple, Katie Anne stood. "Let's get this over with," she said. She put one hand out in front of her as if she were feeling her way to the door.

J. J. stepped aside and followed her faltering footsteps. Putting his hand under her elbow to make sure she didn't fall, he wasn't surprised to feel her trembling. Leaving the girl slumped in the chair by Marlene's desk, he walked down the hall toward Susannah's ruckus as the dispatcher began to ink Katie Anne's fingers.

Once J. J. hauled open the door and walked through, however, Susannah fell silent. She watched him warily as he fished out the right key and fitted it into the lock.

"What have you done with Katie Anne?"

"She's being fingerprinted."

Susannah's arm trembled under his touch as he escorted her through the doorway into the hall. He looked down at the woman. A single tear made its way down through Susannah's ravaged makeup.

"Can I see her now?"

J. J. relented. "I need to get your prints too, then you can both go home. We're ruling people out here, Susannah, not framing them."

"What do you need fingerprints for?"

"To match with the ones from the murder weapon we found outside your back door." J. J. watched Susannah carefully. A boatload of emotions chased across her face: surprise, then anger, and then fear. He felt one eyebrow hitch itself up in surprise.

"Did you put it there?" he asked boldly.

"Of course not!" Susannah snapped back. "What do you take me for? If I'd killed him, would I have put him in my own yard and left the knife by the back door for you to find?"

J. J. didn't have to answer because they'd arrived at Marlene's desk. Katie Anne was futilely trying to wipe the ink from her fingers with a tissue. She didn't look up from her task at her mother's approach.

The front door opened on the other side of Marlene's desk. Dennis and Chaz McFaile stepped inside. One look at the situation and they stopped in their tracks.

Dennis shook off his cousin's restraining arm and resolutely broke eye contact with his former fiancée. "I can save you some trouble, sir. I did it."

Even though J. J. knew exactly what the young man was up to, he was duty bound to take the words at surface value. Of course, that didn't mean that he had to ignore what the young man's words might stir up.

"Is that a fact?" J. J. said, watching the tableau. Susannah was looking at Dennis with fear and loathing, Katie Anne with dismay. There was also a horrified acceptance in her expression that decided J. J. "You'd better step into my office."

J. J. nodded to Marlene, who had things well in hand, having handed Katie Anne a wet towelette to wipe the black from her fingers and who had already pulled Susannah into the chair for her turn with the ink pad. Allowing the two men to precede him into the office, he stepped through and closed the door behind him.

Katie Anne started toward Dennis, but she might have been a fence post for all the notice he took of her.

Chaz propelled his cousin into J. J.'s office. "You can't use that, you know," Chaz stated flatly.

Once seated, Chaz clamped his hand on Dennis's arm and began for him. "My client has some information germane to the investigation into the murder of Greg Whittier."

"So I heard," J. J. said, his voice a low rumble. "Listen up, son. I know what prompted you to say you killed Greg out there. Don't jump into confessing unless you're really guilty. Going to jail for obstruction of justice can be every bit as unpleasant as going to jail for murder."

Dennis looked over at Chaz, who answered for him. "In exchange for this information, I'd like to ask for assurances that any information he gives you will not be held against him in a court of law."

J. J. leaned back in his chair. Forcing himself to smile, he said, "Chaz, you know darned good and well I can't give you any such thing until I know what kind of information we're talking about."

Dennis shifted in his chair and opened his mouth to speak. Chaz said, "Hush, don't make things worse." Dennis closed his mouth and swallowed hard on his words.

"I can give you the murder weapon and who was on the scene at the time," Chaz said coolly.

"Fine," J. J. said, leaning back in his chair. No need to tell them that he already had the murder weapon and a pretty darn good idea of who was on the scene. He wasn't used to being on the opposite side of the fence from Chaz, but he thought he knew how to get around him.

Out of the corner of his eye, J. J. saw Dennis look at Chaz, then look away. Dennis ran his hands over the jeans encasing his thighs and let out a long breath. J. J. smiled. Chaz was probably too young to understand that as long as J. J. pushed against someone like Dennis directly, he was likely to push back in self-defense. With luck, having Chaz here would work in J. J.'s favor.

Chaz copied J. J.'s relaxed sprawl in his chair. His mouth curved in a slow smile to match J. J.'s own. *The son of a gun,* J. J. thought. *His own cousin, and Chaz was having fun. Maybe he wasn't so young after all.*

J. J. decided to spoil Chaz's mood. "All right," he said, leaning forward to rest his right elbow on his knee. Looking Dennis straight in the eye and ignoring Chaz, he asked, "Do you want to start by explaining how your thumbprint came to be on the murder weapon?"

Once again Dennis opened his mouth, and once again Chaz's arm shot out and stopped him. The sour look that Chaz directed at his younger cousin was quite informative, however.

"Listen, Dennis, I can't promise you anything," J. J. said. "But the more you cooperate, the more I'll be in your corner if and when any sentencing occurs. That much I'll gladly give you."

Chaz leaned over and whispered in Dennis's ear.

Dennis sat back, smoothed his jeans yet again, then halt-ingly began his story: "I found him lying at the foot of the front steps at Miss Amilou's."

"I have to ask you: Did you stab Greg?"

"No, it—" Chaz stopped Dennis with a light touch on the sleeve.

J. J. scowled at Chaz. "If it's all the same to you, I would really like to arrest the guilty party sooner rather than later? Dennis says he didn't stab Greg. If he saw someone else there, he needs to tell me. Murder is wrong, no matter who did it and why. I don't care that no one liked Greg. Sally Tucker and her baby—"

Dennis's head jerked up. "She had a baby?"

"She's pregnant with Greg's child."

"So Katie Anne would have—" Dennis bit off whatever it was he was going to say. Chaz turned and gave his cousin a good hard stare.

"So Katie Anne would have . . . ?" J. J. prompted.

"I think my client has answered enough questions for now," Chaz said, one hand firmly clamped on Dennis's arm.

Evidently, Dennis hadn't told Chaz everything. J. J. mea-sured the strength of Chaz's resolve and found himself nod-ding in agreement. "You can use the break room at the end of the hall."

Chaz and Dennis filed out, leaving the door open behind them. J. J. got up to check and see how the fingerprinting session had gone.

Marlene jerked her head toward the ladies' room door. "They're in there, squawking up a storm."

J. J. sauntered closer, where the soft sound of women's voices could be more clearly heard through the grill on the door. These two wouldn't be the first to give testimony while washing their hands.

"If you really want to know, I'm exhausted," Katie Anne replied to Susannah's repeated question. "Instead of stand-ing under the oak tree getting married, I'm washing ink off my fingers because you let that man in our house right before my wedding. What on earth were you thinking?"

"Right now I'm thinking that you're lucky not to be standing under that oak tree marrying a murderer."

"Dennis McFaile is no murderer." Katie Anne's voice rose, yet it lacked conviction. "If anything," she continued, "Greg is the guilty party here. That man ruined my life."

"If you knew him like I knew him, you wouldn't feel like that!"

"If I knew him like you knew him, Mother, it would have been incest."

Katie Anne slammed out of the washroom full tilt into J. J. He looked down at her soft features and bright blue eyes and realized what he should have known all along: Katie Anne was Greg's daughter.

CHAPTER SIXTEEN

KORINE WASN'T SURE what released her from the dream, but she struggled out of bed rather than going back into that hellish nightmare. J. J. had chased Korine around her kitchen table, demanding that she share everything she knew. She had been mute in her dream, but she knew every step that J. J. took brought him closer to forcing her to betray her friend by giving J. J. the evidence he needed to put Amilou in jail.

Draping herself in the chair by the window, Korine reached out and opened the casement window. The heady smell of Amilou's climbing wild rose mingled with the damp of the late-night air. Korine and Amilou had rustled that rose on one of their garden tour trips. They'd felt so daring stealing a snippet of cane at midnight from the shadows of an old Atlanta cemetery. Korine shivered. Had Greg's killer felt that same thrill as she stuck the knife in his heart?

Below her window, a figure moved. She leaned closer, pressing her nose to the dirty screen. The car door made barely a snippet of sound as it closed. If Korine had been asleep, she never would have heard the smooth purr of the Volvo's engine as Amilou pulled out onto the street. The dark shape of the car glided out the drive to the left, toward the center of town.

Four hours later, the car returned. Amilou doused the headlights just before she turned in the drive. Korine had picked up the phone more than once to call Chaz—and had actually dialed the number the last time, getting no answer. Either he and Dennis were sleeping heavily, or neither of them wanted to bother with whoever might be calling at five in the morning.

Korine stumbled on the last step of the narrow, winding

staircase set into a space the size of a broom closet off the kitchen. The hand she instinctively put out to break her fall met the knotty pine of the door at the foot of the steps, which swung open into the kitchen as Amilou softly closed the door behind her to the garage.

The two women stared speechless at one another. Morning's first tendrils of light streaked their faces, obscuring expression.

Amilou was the first to break the silence. "I went out for a walk."

"In your car?" Korine's voice was harsh.

"You've been spying on me?" Amilou threw a sack on the kitchen table.

"I couldn't sleep. Where—"

"Don't ask. That way you won't have to tell." It was Amilou's turn to be harsh. She turned her back to Korine and hung her keys up on the brass hook next to the door.

"We can't help you if you don't tell us what's going on."

Amilou swung around and fumbled with the bag, her stiff back turned to Korine. Picking up the bag, she asked, "Would you mind making the coffee?" as if it were a normal morning. Without turning to see Korine's response, she went into the dining room.

Not sure what to do, Korine flipped the switch on the pot that she'd set up the night before and then followed her. Amilou had put a sheaf of papers in the huge fireplace at the end of the room. She reached up behind the mantel clock and pulled out a box of fireplace matches. She shook one out and leaned down to strike it on the hearth. Korine started forward, but Amilou thrust the burning stick into the fireplace, causing the dry paper to explode into flames.

"Have you lost your mind?" Korine faced Amilou, who stood between her and the fireplace like Cerberus with the flames of hell behind her. This awful confirmation of Korine's worst fears robbed her of her strength. The odd behavior of the last few days was more than grief. The fringe on the rug dug into Korine's bare feet as she stood rooted to the floor, unable to flee, and unable to force herself to rescue the papers from oblivion.

"I told you. This is none of your business."

"You asked me yesterday if I would help you, then you sneak out of the house and tell me it's none of my business. You hired Chaz, and then lied to him. What are you playing at?"

"You want to know where I was the night that Greg died?" Amilou shook from head to toe like she was standing in the path of a blizzard instead of in front of a dying fire. "I was out talking to Sally Tucker." Amilou sank into a ladder-back chair resting against the wall, the back thumping the chair rail with the force of her weight. She avoided Korine's gaze, tracing the new scar in the plaster with her fingertips.

"I didn't know Greg was dead. Sally called that night and said she had to see me. I guess it was about eleven. She said she had something she wanted to show me. You can imagine what I told her."

"But you went?"

"Yes." Amilou pressed her hands on her thighs, holding them still. She looked up at Korine. Pupils wide despite the dimness of the room, she explained: "Sally told me that she had proof that I had conspired to defraud her of an inheritance from my father."

Korine sat, struck dumb by this pronouncement. She'd been right about what Greg had found so fascinating about Sally. He'd always found money to be alluring. "That's what you're burning?" She finally managed to say.

Amilou picked up the poker and stabbed at the smoldering ashes on the grate. "Yes."

"So you're the one who went through Sally's things at the Depot?"

"Yes, I did." Amilou whirled away from the fireplace and came to rest next to Korine. "But for heaven's sake, Korine, you know I would never hurt anyone, not even for the family's sake."

Korine stepped away from the desperation in Amilou's face. She didn't recognize her friend anymore. It was one thing to snip rose canes whose owners were unknown, another thing entirely to steal someone's inheritance, no matter how hateful the beneficiary. She turned her back and stumbled into the kitchen.

Amilou caught up to her before she could wrestle open the back door. Where Korine thought she would go, or what she would do with the information she'd learned, was beyond her understanding. But she did know that she had to get out of that house.

Amilou's hands seized her from behind and spun her in her tracks. Tears streaked Amilou's pale face. "I didn't kill Greg," she repeated. "I loved him. That little bitch did it, I know she did."

"And what makes her your favorite suspect? The fact that she was greedy enough to want whatever part of your inheritance that was rightfully hers?" Korine couldn't keep the words inside any longer.

"She was no more entitled to anything from my family than Greg was, yet they walked off with everything I owned, didn't they? *They* stole from *me*, not the other way around," Amilou said hotly. "I cannot believe you would think that of me."

"So why did you have to burn whatever that was?"

"It only makes a difference to me, Korine. Only to me. Not to Sally Tucker, or to anyone else, not even you." As she spoke, Amilou's voice gradually lost its volume until it faded away entirely.

"I don't believe you." Korine had never thought she could be as angry as she was with Amilou. Yet the words were out, and Korine could never call them back. They hit Amilou with a force that rocked her back on her heels.

Korine hurled another question: "So where were you tonight?"

"I couldn't sleep. I went to see if I could talk to Sally again. She wasn't home, so I came back here."

Korine's eyes burned as she stared, hard, at Amilou. Why could she read Amilou's mind when they were joking around and not even tell if she was telling the truth now. More than anything, Korine wanted to believe that all Amilou was guilty of was nothing more than an inflated sense of family. But then Korine remembered the doused headlights. Amilou was still lying.

"You're an idiot, you know," Korine said grimly. "What you did at the Depot is breaking and entering."

"I know. But not murder."

Korine felt like saying that doing something wrong wasn't excused just because someone had come along and done something worse. She also wanted to fly at Amilou and pound some sense into her. Korine neither said nor did either of those two things. "So when are you going to tell J. J.?"

"I'm not going to tell J. J. anything, and neither should you."

Korine bristled. "If J. J. asks me if you were home all night Thursday, do you expect me to lie?"

"No. I'm not counting on you at all." Amilou looked as betrayed as Korine felt.

"The least you can do is to level with Chaz. As your attorney, he can't really do his best job for you if he's going to have to go around figuring out what you were really up to when you said you were asleep at home."

"I'll tell Chaz," Amilou agreed. She turned, pulled a mug out of the cabinet, and poured herself a cup of coffee. Taking a sip from the blistering brew, she winced and slammed the cup down on the counter.

"It's nearly time to go to church. You'd better go get ready." Amilou's tone was cold and distant. Whatever she'd done, she obviously considered that Korine's behavior constituted desertion to the other side.

"Are you coming?"

"And feel like I'm on parade for the whole town to see? No, thank you."

"Suit yourself." Korine hesitated, then pulled open the door to the stair, ducking her head so that she wouldn't hit her head on the low lintel over the steps. She didn't bother to close the door behind her. A last glance over her shoulder before the turning steps took her out of sight showed Amilou, her hands braced against the sink, head bowed between stiff shoulders.

Korine turned her back and continued on her way. She felt weak as a kitten, barely able to lift one foot in front of the other. More than anything, she wanted their relationship restored to where it had been before Greg and Sally came back to town. It wasn't that easy. Amilou was going to have to come to terms with what she'd done on her own.

When Marlene called early Sunday morning with an urgent call for J. J., he assumed that it was about Dennis's confession and booking the night before. It wasn't. "You know how Jett went over to take the crime-scene tape down at The Depot this morning? Well, he called and told me to get you over there. He's found Sally Tucker."

"Thanks, Marlene. Has Leon checked in yet?"

"No, but—"

J. J. cut her off. "I know full well he's not due on till three this afternoon. I need him in there now."

"Chief—"

"I don't have time to talk much about it now, but we're going to have to talk soon. I know it's not my business, but you're going to want to take some time off."

"Thanks, I think." Marlene's voice was sour.

J. J. replaced the receiver.

"Who was that?" Janey's sleepy voice asked from the other side of the bed.

"Marlene. They've found Sally. Maybe now I can get some real answers."

Sitting up, the sheet stretched across her chest, Janey looked thoughtful as she answered him. "I don't suppose she'll confess. It would make things so much easier."

"Maybe for you," J. J. said, leaning over to kiss his beautiful wife good-bye. "But we've already got one confession I don't think will stand the test of time and evidence. We don't need another one unless it's real."

J. J. skidded into the parking lot at The Depot. Gravel still flying, he put the cruiser in park. Jett met him inside the front door.

"How many times do I need to tell you not to leave a suspect alone who's got a history of scampering?"

"She's not going anywhere." Jett held open the door to Sally's room. "In here."

The room was once again the scene of a crime. But this time, it was far more serious than breaking and entering. Wrapped in a white satin sheet on the bed was the still body of Sally Tucker.

"Jett, lord love a duck, tell someone when you find a body so we can hurry up a little more," J. J. said, straightening.

"I told Marlene, sir."

"Well, she never—" J. J. remembered cutting Marlene off when she tried to tell him something more about Jett's call. "Oh, hell, call Marlene and tell her to keep this to herself." He reconsidered. "I'll do it. You carry on here, I'll send Leon over when I find his sorry . . . quit looking at me like that." J. J. scowled at Jett's raised eyebrows as if it was Jett's fault that Sally had gotten herself killed before J. J. had a chance to talk to her.

The fact was that it left J. J. with a bunch of nothing. Dennis may have confessed to killing Greg, but he couldn't have done this. From the look of the body, J. J. would put the time of death at sometime during the night. Dennis was locked up tighter than Dick's hatband down at the jail. Chances were, there was only one killer in Pine Grove.

At least it would get Katie Anne off his doorstep when he let Dennis go. She'd been camping outside his office door ever since Dennis confessed. She'd even gone so far as to try and confess herself. There were so many holes in her story that J. J. had told her to stop wasting his time. At least he got to cross the girl off his list.

Jett's eyebrows hadn't relaxed. "I just found her, sir. Don't kill the messenger."

J. J.'s scowl deepened. Just what he needed was a wiseacre in charge of his second murder scene in three days. He needed Leon on the job. J. J. slammed out of the room. On the way by the desk, he helped himself to the phone and called Marlene. Predictably enough, there was no answer.

CHAPTER SEVENTEEN

THE PINE GROVE METHODIST CHURCH'S quiet stone facade had been in place since it was built in 1857. The stained glass windows reflected the heart of its members. Clear reds, blues, greens, and yellows, muted gold, and brilliant purple sent rainbows of color across the sanctuary. There were panels dedicated to many of the county's big families.

The opening organ salute relaxed the muscles in Korine's neck for the first time in days. Her face turned immediately to the small window near her seat. It was dedicated to the farmers of the region, given by a family who now raised Christmas trees just outside town.

Rather than the usual cross or dove or Bible story, this one's picture was unique. A sheaf of wheat surrounded by a halo of light represented the hardworking settlers who had built this house of worship.

Some people didn't like the odd window. There had even been a movement at one time to take it out. Korine was glad they hadn't. To her, the life-giving food at the center of the window and the rain falling from the dark cloud at the top were two of God's greatest gifts.

Edward Richardson climbed to his pulpit. Several hymns and verses later, Korine settled in to listen to his sermon. A lovely man, he always seemed to pick what was uppermost in Korine's mind for his sermon topic. That morning, she found it impossible to concentrate on the message. About the third sentence, she found her attention smack dab back on the topic that she had come to church to avoid.

Yes, Amilou had still loved Greg after all the petty little things he had done to make her life miserable. While Korine would have never stood for it herself, she understood that others might make a different choice. Yet, despite Amilou's semi-logical explanation of her nocturnal errand on the night that Greg died, more issues were raised than laid to rest. There was an undercurrent present in Amilou's tone and words that morning that Korine couldn't put her finger on.

She shifted in her seat and placed her hymnal back in the pocket in front of her. In addition to the part of the Amilou/Greg story that Korine couldn't fathom, there was the issue of Sally Tucker. Korine now knew what Sally had been doing in the courthouse Wednesday.

Korine wanted to trust her friend, but once trust was broken in a relationship, it was pretty nearly impossible to mend. A stray comment from the sermon penetrated her daze.

"Who are we to cast stones?" the Reverend demanded. He shook his fist somewhere in the direction of Sarah Jane on the opposite side of the sanctuary, but Korine knew he was really speaking to her. She squirmed in her seat yet again, causing the casual acquaintance sitting next to her to lean over and inquire about her health.

She was so fixed on hurting because Amilou had lied to her, yet Korine herself had convicted Amilou in her own heart of killing Greg. The fact that Amilou wasn't acting like herself was no excuse. Korine bowed her head and fumbled a brief prayer of forgiveness as the minister took his seat.

The collection plate passed by. Thankful for the disruption to her morbid thoughts, she dropped her weekly envelope in. Looking across the aisle, she saw Nicki sitting up a few rows.

As the final notes of the closing hymn rang forth, Nicki turned and wiggled her fingers at Korine. Even as Korine nodded and made "let's meet" motions with her hands, she felt the sick feeling grow in her stomach. She needed to talk with Nicki to see if she could continue to fill in. The way things were looking, Dirty Women would be needing an extra pair of hands to replace Amilou—or Korine. Nicki returned the nod with a smile.

As they filed out, Korine hung back to intercept Nicki. "I

need to talk to you sometime today. When would be a good time?"

"Is it about Dennis?" Nicki asked, her arm going solicitously around Korine's shoulders.

"What do you mean?"

"I heard that Katie Anne turned Dennis in last night."

"What are you talking about?"

"I forgot, you spent the night with Amilou, so you wouldn't know. Dennis is in jail."

"J. J. can't arrest Dennis. He didn't do anything really wrong."

"*Really* wrong? What sort of wrong thing did he do, Korine?"

Korine felt as if Nicki had kicked her in the stomach, but instead of knocking the wind out of her as it should have done, she felt as if a restriction around her diaphragm was eased. "I've got to go."

"I'm sorry to be the one to tell you. Go on." Nicki gave Korine a swift hug, then released her to the swarm of people emptying into the parking lot.

Thrusting Amilou back in a corner of her mind, Korine went out and got into her car.

J. J. found Katie Anne asleep outside his office door when he returned from The Depot. He resisted the urge to slam the door as he went by. It wasn't the girl's fault that he had a second murder to investigate. Of course, he did consider it her fault that he had less than three hours' sleep under his hat.

The latest report from the lab lay on his desk. J. J. read it through and resisted the urge to open his window and toss the whole thing out. Instead, he opened the case file folder and slid the papers out onto the mess on top of his desk. He gave himself a few moments to arrange them to his satisfaction, then he picked up the phone and dialed.

"Are you willing to do a deal with your cousin?"

"What?" Chaz's groggy voice said.

"Good morning, Sleeping Beauty. Deal. Dennis."

"What kind of deal?"

"Limited sentence plus probation and community service for moving the body and the murder weapon in return for testifying where he found the body, the weapon, and who he saw there."

"I'll be right over."

J. J. spent the next half hour staring at the evidence sheets on his desk. Now that he knew that Dennis moved the body, he had a pretty good idea who had killed Greg. Things would have fallen into place if it weren't for Sally's murder. Marlene rang through to tell him that Chaz had arrived and was waiting with Dennis.

J. J. slid the papers back inside the file folder before shutting it in the bottom drawer. Fishing the keys out of his pocket, he opened his office door and let it slam behind him. He heard Katie Anne scramble up and hurry after him as he walked toward the lockup in the back.

As the locked door swung shut behind him, J. J. glanced back. Katie Anne had her nose pressed to the glass of the door like a child at a pet shop window. She'd get Dennis back soon enough. J. J. wanted a little chat with that young man before he let him go.

It was lunchtime before the three men walked out of the room together. Dennis turned back to shake J. J.'s hand before going to pick up his belongings. "Thank you, sir. I promise not to disappoint you in this."

"Son, your Aunt Korinc's told you time and again to think more and react less. That's a true piece of advice. Don't hesitate to take it."

"I'll call Amilou and ask her to come in." Chaz didn't look nearly as happy as Dennis.

"You do that. She's got a whole lot of explaining to do here."

Chaz grimaced, then went down the hall to pick up the phone.

As J. J. escorted Dennis out the door of the room he'd used for the interview, Katie Anne planted herself in their way. She took a few steps back, giving Dennis enough room to make it out the door.

Dennis stopped, his hand on the doorknob. "Chief Bascom said that you were here all night bugging him about letting me go."

"I couldn't let you go to jail. You didn't hurt anyone."

"I may have to go to jail for a little while, for burying him." Dennis didn't look at his former fiancée, focusing instead on the list of Most Wanted on the wall behind her.

"It doesn't matter to me," Katie Anne said, as if the slightest wrong move on her part would scare Dennis away. "I'll be here when you come home. Would you still have me?"

Dennis inhaled, a deep cleansing breath. "You should know that I had to tell Chief Bascom about your mom."

"I know." She took a step closer. "Is that why they let you go?"

"Partly, but something else has happened. They're bringing in Amilou Whittier."

J. J. cleared his throat. The pair in front of him jumped. "If you'll excuse me, I'll leave you two to talk. Feel free to use this room if you want to."

Dennis nodded his thanks and pulled Katie Anne through the door as if afraid that she might change her mind and run away again. As the door swung shut behind them, J. J. caught a glimpse of Katie Anne raising her face to meet Dennis's kiss.

Thank goodness at least one thing was turning out right in the whole mess. J. J. turned his back on the couple and trudged down the hall to check and see if Chaz had anything to say about Amilou.

Katie Anne and Dennis were exiting the police station as Korine started up the front steps.

"What on earth happened?" Korine put her hands on her hips. She didn't know whether to be angry that Dennis hadn't called her, or relieved that J. J. had let him go. The fact that Katie Anne was by his side had not escaped her notice either. "I thought Chaz was going in with you to keep you from being put into jail?"

"Can we go someplace else to talk about this, Aunt Korine?"

"I can't believe J. J. kept you all night. Didn't you have the sense to call Chaz to come and bail you out?"

Chaz chose that moment to swing open the glass door behind Dennis. Korine saw him hesitate, then continue on down the steps toward the group on the sidewalk.

"Mother, before you say anything"—he held his hand up and halted the question Korine had been about to blurt out—"I have to go bring Amilou in for more questioning. They finally found Sally Tucker. She was killed sometime last night."

"Last night?" Korine repeated faintly.

"Thank goodness you stayed over with Amilou, Mom. At least she's got an alibi this time around."

Korine hesitated too long to say anything to Chaz about Amilou's second nocturnal excursion. He must have taken her silence for agreement, because he hugged her. Then he walked over to his car and got in.

"Miss Korine?" Katie Anne's soft voice reached into the fog surrounding Korine's brain.

"Yes, dear?" she replied automatically.

"Would you mind taking us home?"

Korine focused on the pale little face of the young woman standing close by her side. "Certainly. I'd be happy to. But first, would you mind stopping to get some lunch? I'm famished."

What she really needed was time to think. Certainly, she didn't want to be home, available for J. J. to question about Amilou's alibi. "This way," she said, and tucked her arm through Dennis's.

Conversation stopped at the Green Whistle when Korine, Dennis, and Katie Anne walked through the door. Juanita June hurried over to greet them.

"Is it true?"

"Which rumor?" Korine asked dryly.

"The 'Sally's dead' rumor."

"Evidently so." Korine had enough time on the way over to regain some measure of calm.

"You want your usual table?" Juanita June asked Katie Anne.

Katie Anne grinned and said, "Yes, please, but hold the napkins."

Juanita June grinned back, leaving Korine to exchange puzzled glances with Dennis as they followed the pair back to the far corner booth.

Juanita June poured out coffee for all of them, took their orders, then scurried away to deliver an armful of plates to the mayor and his wife. Korine returned Sarah Jane's wave halfheartedly. She was grateful to Hank for putting out a restraining hand when Sarah Jane looked to be coming over.

Bringing the coffee cup to her lips, Korine took a long welcome sip. The three of them sat in silence until their food came. The night's watch by the window, followed by her bitter disappointment with Amilou's lies that morning, had sapped all Korine's energy.

Katie Anne pushed her french fries around on the plate with her left hand, while tightly clutching Dennis's hand with the right. Korine frowned. Katie Anne's ring finger on the left hand was still bare. Although, if the way the two of them were looking at each other was any indication, they'd soon be married anyway.

"Dennis, why don't you give the girl back her ring?"

Katie Anne dropped Dennis's hand.

Dennis captured Katie's Anne's hand in his again.

"It's okay. I can't be too upset," Dennis said. "I lost a murder weapon; losing an engagement ring can't be any harder than that."

"What do you mean, 'losing an engagement ring'?" Korine asked.

"I threw the ring away the other night and can't find it."

"Threw it away?"

"Long story. I went looking for it, which got me picked up by the police. If that crazy woman who owns the house finds it, I'll bet she keeps it. I probably should have waited for morning, but I wasn't thinking clearly at the time." She and Dennis exchanged a long look. Both of them leaned toward each other, like magnets set in alignment.

"Have you tried a metal detector?"

Katie Anne's mouth opened in an *O* of delight. "What a great idea."

As coolly as he had dismissed the loss of the ring before, Dennis moved quickly on Korine's idea. He got up, dragging Katie Anne along with him. "Mr. Reynolds has one we can borrow."

"Do you mind if we leave you here?" Katie Anne asked over her shoulder.

"Go on," Korine urged. "I'll meet you at home. Good luck." She spoke to the couple's retreating backs. Settling back against the seat, she surveyed the room.

Abruptly, she got up and fished enough money out of her purse to settle the bill and tossed it on the table. Sitting still, alone with her morbid thoughts, was not a good idea right now. Korine wanted to be home, on her knees, dirt under her fingernails, working in her beloved garden. There, she knew that she could figure out what to do.

CHAPTER EIGHTEEN

AMILOU LOOKED LIKE HELL, J. J. thought. Her hands kept alternately smoothing and ruffling her hair. Chaz looked no better at her side. He'd asked for a few moments alone with his client. "To bring her up to speed," he'd said.

Both had emerged from the conference room looking shaken. J. J. knew he had to press hard this time. "So Korine was there last night. Did the two of you go anywhere?"

"No." A sigh escaped from Amilou. "Do we have to go over all this again?"

Before answering, J. J. fiddled with some papers on his desk, then relaunched his question. "Where were you last night?"

"At home, trying to sleep."

"So you were awake?"

"It's hard to sleep when your husband's been murdered," Amilou snapped. Her beige foundation, presumably smeared on to cover the dark circles under her eyes, just served to accentuate their dusky color.

"Did you leave your house at all last night?" J. J. repeated.

Without hesitating, Amilou said, "No. I did not."

Chaz patted her arm. Amilou gave him a look in return that caused him to pull back.

"Were you aware of where Sally Tucker was staying?"

"You know I was!" Amilou snapped.

J. J. waited. She didn't volunteer anything more. After a full minute, he asked another question. "What were you doing at The Depot Thursday night?"

"What?" Amilou's voice was faint.

"Thursday night, around midnight, you were seen going into The Depot. One of the guests was up looking for a book to read and heard the front door open and close and saw you go in. He later heard raised voices coming out of Sally Tucker's room."

Amilou looked at Chaz and he nodded in return. His face, however had grown into a stern mask unlike any expression J. J. had ever seen him wear.

"Sally called. She asked me to come over. Said she had kicked Greg out and that she had something to show me."

"What was it?"

"I don't know. When I got there, her room was torn to bits. I'm not stupid, you know. I figured that I'd be blamed, so I left. Before anyone saw me. At least I thought I did," she added in a bitter afterthought."

"Amilou, I hate to have to do this, but your fingerprints were found in that room. I'm going to have to ask you to stay with us for a while."

"You mean arrest her?" Chaz sounded incredulous. "You can't do that, she's got an alibi for last night. You keep saying that you can't imagine the two cases aren't linked."

"I'm arresting her for breaking and entering. The witness clearly stated that Amilou was inside The Depot for an hour." J. J. turned back to Amilou and stared at her. She wouldn't meet his look, fiddling instead with the clasp on her purse.

"I wish you hadn't've lied to me." J. J. said.

Amilou looked up. "I wish you could believe me," she said quietly. Janey might as well have been standing in the room between them. It would hurt her as much as it did Amilou and J. J. that things were the way they were.

He began the rigmarole of citing Amilou her rights. She sat, hands clasped in her lap, eyes wide open, yet closed to thought.

As J. J. finished she shook her head slightly and stood. "Which way do I go?"

"I'll show you."

Chaz reached over and hugged Amilou. She pushed him away, but more gently this time than when she had repudiated him earlier. "It's going to be all right," Chaz soothed.

"You're doing fine, honey. Don't feel bad." Amilou turned to

J. J. "Would it be okay if I wrote a little note to Korine. There are some things she'll need to attend to for me if I'm going to spend any time here."

J. J. handed her a pen and a piece of paper. "Chaz, you okay with this?"

"It's just gardening instructions, J. J., not a confession."

"I knew that."

Despite the situation, Amilou looked up at J. J. from under her lashes. Their eyes met, and he felt a flicker of amusement pass between them, as if the interview had never taken place. For a moment, they were just two friends, sharing a private joke.

The moment died quickly. Amilou handed the note to Chaz and walked out the door, J. J. following close behind.

Korine shifted the knee pad over to the left and pulled out another straggling clump of chickweed. Pitched over her shoulder, it joined a small mountain of roots-up plants lying on a tarp. This bed should have been weeded a month ago. Now, it might not recover from its scratched-out look before winter. Throwing her spade down in the dirt in disgust, she rocked back off her knees and stood.

She gathered the four corners of the tarp and dragged it over to the compost heap. Emptying it into the bin, she debated for the umpteenth time what she knew about Amilou.

Amilou had been genuinely surprised and shocked when she found Greg's body. Knowing that Dennis had moved him, Amilou's surprise lost its significance.

Amilou hated Sally, yet went to see her at The Depot. That was the day that Sally's room was broken into and savaged.

Amilou had asked Korine to spend the night, but then secretly left the house in the middle of the night. The next morning, Sally was found dead.

Korine pressed both hands against the pine boards surrounding the pile of discarded plants, grass clippings, and last autumn's leaves. That reporter had been right. Korine wondered who her source had been. Probably Susannah.

Although Sally was also a possibility.

The sound of Chaz's car returning home roused her. She pressed herself up from the bin. A sharp pain in her hand made her cry out.

"What have you done now, Mother?" Chaz asked as he climbed out of the car.

"Splinter, I think," Korine said, searching her palm. Rubbing it on her jeans, she decided she needed more than reading glasses. She could feel it but couldn't see anything at all.

"Let me have a look." Chaz seized her hand and ran his smooth thumb over the pads. Pausing for an instant, he nipped the splinter out with the tweezers from his pocket-knife.

"Always the Boy Scout," Korine said dryly, rubbing her finger over the sore spot.

"I didn't do very well for Amilou this time. J. J.'s arrested her."

Korine froze. "Did she tell him about going to The Depot?"

"He already knew. There was a witness who identified her as being the one who was in Sally's room arguing for over an hour Thursday night." Chaz shook his head as he walked slowly next to Korine up the steps. "Mom, has she told you anything more about what it was that Sally called her about?"

"Suppose you tell me what she told you, then I'll tell you if she's lying again."

Chaz's expression remained neutral, but Korine still knew when her son was upset.

"I can't help being angry," she said. "I know she's my best friend, but she's lied to us all along about this. She owed me more than that."

"And what do you suppose she'll feel like, knowing that you've been going around checking up on her." Chaz's words lashed Korine's already frayed nerves. "You knew she was lying and you never called her on it. Instead, you made up your mind that she was guilty and then went around trying to find evidence to support your supposition. Well, I happen to think she didn't kill either of those two people, and I aim to prove it, with or without your help."

"Chaz, I—"

"Here." Chaz thrust his hand in his pocket and pulled out a crumpled piece of paper. "Amilou had some instructions for you and Janey about Dirty Women." He shook his head and walked away in disgust.

Korine looked down at the paper her son had thrust into her hand:

To whom it may concern:

I hereby give my ownership interest in Three Dirty Women to Korine McFaile and Janey Bascom of my own free will, with my everlasting thanks for their friend-ship and support.

Amilou Pierce Whittier

Korine felt a stab of pain in her chest as the tears began. Chaz was more than grown, he was right.

"Wait," Korine called after her son. "Tell me what I can do to help."

Chaz's tall form hesitated in the doorway to the kitchen, then turned back toward his mother. "Let's sit down and talk about it, shall we?" he asked, holding the door open for her.

Korine recognized that the sour taste of betrayal in her mouth was created more by her own deeds rather than Amilou's false words. She followed Chaz into the kitchen and began to listen to his plan.

"I don't know what to think." J. J. leaned forward in his chair so that Janey could get to his lower back. "Other than you give the best backrubs in the whole world."

"Pulling weeds strengthens hands. Korine calls it 'Hoe-Bo.'"

"She would. Speaking of Korine, she wasn't answering her phone at all today."

"I know. She didn't come by Amilou's either." Her hands

paused in their movement. "What will happen to Amilou for tossing around Sally's things?

"Honey," J. J. swiveled around in his chair and traced a finger around the line of her jaw. "It was more than tossing. She shredded every scrap of clothing the woman owned. Furniture was broken. Frankly, I have no idea how Sally got out in one piece."

"Did you know that Amilou paid for the lawyer that got the restraining order on Raynell? I never would have been able to leave him without her."

"Don't sell yourself short. You did the work there, not Amilou, not Korine. You." J. J. leaned forward and captured Janey's face between his hands. "I know how much this hurts you. It hurts me almost as badly to have to put a friend in jail. At least I haven't had to charge her with murder, although it may yet come to that."

Janey walked away from J. J., hands balled at her sides. J. J. got up and went to stand behind her, watching her reflection in the window.

"Want a divorce yet?" he asked lightly, trying to mask the dismay and fear he felt winding its way around his middle section.

Janey turned and clasped her arms around him. "You will not get out of this that easily, Johnny Joe Bascom, Junior."

J. J. winced. He hated his full name, so hokey sounding. Still, he hugged her back. "I have an idea; do you suppose you could help me again? Like you did yesterday with Katie Anne."

"I suppose so. Not," she added hastily, "that I want to do it all the time. Keep that want ad running."

J. J. watched a blue jay dive-bomb the bird feeder by the window, driving all the smaller birds away.

"Do you mind if I ask you a question?" Janey hooked her thumbs through the loops of J. J.'s pants while she waited for his answer.

"Sure," he said. "Go ahead and ask. I might not be able to answer, but you can ask."

She loosened one hand and used it to tease the gray hair

starting in at his temples. "If Amilou has an alibi for last night, why do you think she's guilty?"

"You told me yourself that *anyone* is capable of murder. Have you changed your mind?"

"I suppose I have. There's not been enough anger in Amilou over the past few days to go killing someone else. Just grief. I don't think she killed Sally."

"Who else would want to kill her?'

"I don't know." Janey's answer was almost a wail. "That's why I want you to keep that want ad running, so I don't have to think about that sort of thing." The timer buzzed on the stove. She went over to pull out the frozen dinners.

Over the Salisbury steak and mashed potatoes, J. J. watched the play of emotions on his wife's face. Finally, not able to stand it anymore, he said, "What is going through your mind?"

Looking slightly guilty, Janey said, "You never answered my question."

"I had to arrest her for the Breaking and Entering. As I said, I don't like the idea, but I may have to charge her with murder too. I just won't know until I get more information."

"Like talking to Korine?"

"If she'll ever return my phone calls. I may have to pick her up just to get answers to my questions."

"Susannah's been acting awfully strange lately." Janey speared a forkful of potatoes and lifted them to her mouth. "Ruthie Lee told me this morning in the Safeway that she heard Susannah bought an odd sort of dress to wear as the mother of the bride."

"What kind of dress is odd for a mother of the bride?"

"Ruthie Lee said that Mary Faye told her she saw Susannah leaving that fancy new dress shop over on First Street with a tea-length ivory dress."

"Doesn't sound too odd to me. That sounds like Susannah picking up Katie Anne's dress. Garden wedding, remember? She'd have a heck of a grass stain pulling a train along the grass."

"I hadn't thought of that." Janey conceded the point.

"I know," J. J. said glumly, stacking the paper trays to toss in the garbage pail. "That's my problem. I can think of reasonable things to explain away everyone's behavior in this case."

"Except that murder isn't reasonable. Sooner or later, you'll find the thing that can't be explained. Then you'll have the right person."

"Thanks for your vote of confidence," J. J. said dryly. "Now I've got to go back to the office and see if I can't find that thing that can't be explained."

"Wait a minute. You said you needed my help?"

"I want to check out one more thing before enlisting you. Would you mind waiting up for me?"

Janey nodded her reluctant agreement. J. J. picked his hat up off the worn Formica counter and set it on his head. He could feel her staring at him as he walked out the back door. For her sake, he would look long and hard to find something that would exonerate her friend. But if he found evidence that would convict Amilou for murder, he wouldn't ignore it.

CHAPTER NINETEEN

KORINE STEPPED OUT OF HER CAR early Monday morning in front of the Cut 'n Curl. Ruthie Lee waved from inside the shop as she turned the closed sign around. Korine wasn't sure why she had kept her regular appointment when there were so many other more important things to do. She'd gotten in her car expecting to go to the courthouse. The car's autopilot took over and delivered her to her hair appointment instead.

Well, she thought, *as long as I'm here.* She unhooked her seat belt, picked up her purse, and disembarked from the car. The courthouse didn't open till ten, and she had to look decent for the funeral, even if it was going to be the worst occasion of her life.

Sarah Jane Jenkins stepped out of the car next to Korine's. Sarah Jane's foot hadn't hit the ground before she started to talk. "Such goings-on. Sure am glad my hair appointment is today or I'd've never looked right for this funeral."

Korine had tried several times to switch her hair appointment so that she wouldn't have to share company with the biggest gossip in town. Somehow, Sarah Jane always managed to change her time to match Korine's. Amilou had finally pointed out to Korine that Sarah Jane just wanted to have her hair done at the same time to have an opportunity to pump her for information. It was that darned propensity people had of confiding in her that made Korine so attractive to Sarah Jane; she thought Korine was a kindred spirit. The two of them entered the shop together.

"Morning," Ruthie Lee said. "Sarah Jane, you just have a seat while I get started with Korine."

Ruthie Lee flipped the black plastic cape open and

snapped it around Korine's neck. A few blissful minutes later, after a shampoo and a head and neck massage, Korine sat in the chair as Ruthie Lee pumped it up to her height.

"What time's the funeral?" Ruthie Lee asked.

"Four o'clock," Sarah Jane answered, before Korine could even open her mouth. Korine looked at Ruthie Lee in the mirror, and both rolled their eyes. One of the many things that Korine had to do that day was to talk with Ruthie Lee about when Sally and Amilou had their dustup in the Cut 'n Curl. She kicked herself for missing the opportunity to use the relative privacy of the shampoo corner instead of asking in front of Sarah Jane. Still, Korine reconsidered, for once Sarah's presence might come in handy.

"How well did you know Sally Tucker?" Korine asked.

"I cut her hair for her," Ruthie Lee said. "But Sarah Jane knew her mother, didn't you?"

"Lived next door to her for eleven years," Sarah Jane sniffed.

"So you knew Sally growing up?"

"Sweet little girl. I tried to provide a good example for her, but you couldn't expect she'd grow up any better than her mother." Sarah Jane delivered this chilling epitaph with a surprising amount of self-satisfaction.

"And I'm sure you told her how hard she'd need to work to overcome her handicap." Try as she might, Korine was not able to keep her tone from being tart.

Sarah Jane tilted her face so that she could stare assessingly over the top of her glasses at Korine. "Actually, I managed to keep that to myself, thank you. Just as I've managed to keep a few other things to myself over the years."

Korine had a sudden and distinct memory of Charlie relating the epic story of how he and Hank, long before he thought of becoming mayor of Pine Grove, had climbed the water tower one summer night and painted it. Sarah Jane Jenkins had been waiting for them at the bottom. She'd never told. What she had done was to force them to volunteer to repaint it when the vandalism was discovered. Blackmail, but appropriate blackmail. She wasn't sure what it said about Hank that he'd later married the woman.

Korine looked at Sarah Jane with fresh eyes. She might very well be helpful. "What was Sally's childhood like that she had so far to go?"

"Humph," Sarah Jane replied.

"Maybelle Tucker was a fast one," Ruthie Lee chimed in. "I remember her from school. All the boys wanted to date her. She settled down after we graduated, though. I remember hearing some of the boys lamenting that fact."

"Didn't she work for Judge Pierce before he died? Amilou's father?" Korine asked.

"She was Judge Pierce's assistant," Sarah Jane said shortly.

The scissors snipped a little close to Korine's ear. She flinched. A shower of gray hair fluttered to the floor like washed-out whirlybirds. Korine met the startled gaze of Ruthie Lee in the mirror in front of her.

"Oops."

"I never thought I'd hear you say that word," Korine said, closing her eyes, afraid to see how bald she was on that side.

"Nothing we can't fix," Ruthie Lee said, leaning close to Korine's ear to inspect the damage. "You know how we've been talking about going with that new style?"

Korine glared at herself in the mirror. She wasn't bald, but the right side was now missing a considerable chunk of hair. She sighed. "Go ahead. Chaz didn't pay you to do that, did he?" The suspicion in her voice caused Ruthie Lee's ready laugh to emerge.

"No, no. I was just thinking of something else, that's all. Funny wasn't it," Ruthie Lee said, the scissors snipping close to Korine's other ear. "That both Sally and her mother worked for men like that."

Korine glanced over at Sarah Jane and was rewarded with seeing her lips pursed in the fashion they so often assumed before Sarah Jane dropped a choice piece of gossip. However, the mean look in her eyes told Korine that after Korine's smart comment, Sarah Jane wouldn't willingly part with any information. For a change, Korine wished that Sarah Jane would open her mouth.

"Men like that?" Korine repeated.

Ruthie Lee stopped, her comb arrested in midair. "You know," she said, her other hand waving the scissors in a circle. "Men. Like that."

All of sudden, it tumbled. Amilou's tight voice replayed in her head, speaking of her father. Korine thought that perhaps she realized what made Sally Tucker think she had a right to The Pines.

"Never mind that," Korine said, pushing away the blow dryer in Ruthie Lee's hands. "I've got to go to the courthouse."

"It's only nine," Sarah Jane said. "Why the all-fired hurry?"

"I promised Dennis I'd do something for him," Korine lied.

"He got the license already." Sarah Jane flipped a page in the *People* magazine open on her lap.

Ruthie Lee turned the blow dryer on full blast and Korine didn't bother replying. When she was finished, Ruthie Lee whirled Korine around to face the mirror. A total stranger looked back at her. Soft feathers of hair reached down to grace Korine's cheeks and forehead. She put a hand up to see if it was really her that looked like a million dollars.

She slid out of the chair carefully, still a little wary that a sudden movement would ruin this sophisticated new look. Pulling twice the usual tip out of her bag, she slipped it onto the shelf next to the curlers.

As Korine faced Ruthie Lee across the cash register, she took the last opportunity she would get to ask what had happened between Amilou and Sally: "I heard Sally was in the other day."

"Yes, although not to get her hair done." Ruthie Lee looked up at Korine through her bangs. "Amilou was here too. I thought for a while we were going to have a catfight right here."

"But you didn't?"

"Well, it started out that way. But since I'm still making payments on that new window I had to put in when Imogene drove through it without insurance, I made them leave." She lowered her voice so that Sarah Jane couldn't hear. "I saw them later, talking real quiet over by the post office." Ruthie Lee nodded once, looking sage.

"Talking, did you say?" Sarah Jane asked, coming up to the register.

"Yes, I'm trying to talk some sense into Amilou and have her come stay with me for a while," Korine said.

"She'll never do that. That old house means more to her than people do. She's a cold fish if you ask me."

Korine hadn't asked. But on one thing they were in agreement. A house, even an old family homestead, wasn't worth what Amilou might have done.

Korine eased into a parking place right at ten o'clock. The air-conditioning unit up in Judge Carrolton's office was already dripping on the sidewalk underneath her window. As a matter of course, Korine ran a practiced eye over the tired-looking shrubs cowering in front of the red brick building. Perhaps a word in the right ear at the Garden Club would get something done about the eyesore.

She put her hand on the chipped paint on the massive door handle. There had been rumors that the county wanted to tear this old building down and build a modern concrete-faced structure to take its place. Over her dead body. She ignored the gleam of brass peering out from under the dead black paint. She had to find out if Sally really was who Korine thought she was.

She pushed through the swinging doors to the county clerk's office. Sarah Jane was there before her, looking confused and angry.

"Frieda, get back out here right now. Are you avoiding me?" There was more than a trace of hurt mixed in with the anger in Sarah Jane's voice.

An indistinct sound of distress came from around the half-closed door to the records room behind the desk. Frieda appeared. Her lips were extremely swollen, her skin a vile tomato color that clashed horribly with the orange rinse she'd used on her hair.

"My word!" Sarah Jane said.

"His lip oak— Ow," The apparition said unintelligibly, obviously in a great deal of pain.

"What on earth happened to you?"

Frieda picked up a pencil and wrote a note: "The ship broke down. We spent fourteen hours on a loading dock in Miami waiting for a part. This is your fault!!!"

Sarah Jane looked ready to spit nails. "What do you mean, the ship broke down and it's all my fault. You told me that you couldn't get tickets."

"You need to be at the doctor's, not here," Korine said decisively, to head off trouble. "What are you thinking of?"

Frieda pulled the paper back toward her and wrote, "All I do at home is cry, so I came to work."

Sarah Jane said, "Sounds like all you're doing here is crying. My fault? You went without me, didn't you?"

Korine said, "I think she's already paid the price for leaving you at home. Next time *you* can go without *her*. Maybe you should be feeling grateful that both of you aren't sitting here looking miserable instead of just your friend."

Sarah Jane turned on her heel and walked out, not looking at all grateful.

Frieda pushed a typed note toward Korine that said, "What can I do for you?"

"Sally Tucker was in here last week. Do you remember what she wanted?"

Frieda shrugged, then exclaimed in pain. "She wanted her birth certificate," she wrote on the pad.

Korine felt a tightness begin in her chest. "May I see it?"

Frieda pointed to the price list under the glass of the countertop. She disappeared into the back room as Korine fished in her purse for her wallet. She pulled out a crisp twenty-dollar bill and laid it on the counter. After several very long minutes, Frieda came back, her hands empty. If her face had been capable of showing emotion, it would have to have been confusion.

"It's not there. I filed it back on Thursday morning. I'll look. Will call when I find it," Frieda scribbled.

Korine wouldn't hold her breath, but she didn't say anything about that. She scooped up her twenty from the countertop and filed it back in her wallet. Her feet dragged as she walked toward the door.

She pulled the doorknob, only to find that it came off in her hand. Jimmy, the ancient courthouse maintenance man, poked his head in the door. "Miss Korine, this place is fallin' apart." He shook his head sorrowfully. "Miss Frieda came in this morning and told me how her lock wasn't working anymore. Judge Carrolton keeps talkin' about gettin' a new place put up. Maybe it's time."

"The lock wasn't working?" Korine asked. All weekend she'd waited to get in and she could have waltzed in anytime.

"No ma'am. It's sheered off right here." Jimmy held up a short length of a brass bolt. Korine looked at it more closely. The decorative brass showed through the black paint on the lock as it had on the front doors, but more interestingly, it was clearly made by a sharp object rather than by wear and tear.

"Thank you, Jimmy," Korine said and went back to ask one more thing of Frieda.

"I've got another request. Do you have copies of probated wills?"

Frieda nodded.

"Can I see a copy of Judge Pierce's?"

Eyes wide, Frieda backed into the file room. Korine could hear the slamming of drawers, then the whirring of the copy machine.

She came out with an envelope and took Korine's money.

Scribbling another note, Frieda shoved it across the desk. "I forgot, Sally took a copy of this too."

"Thanks," Korine said, her words hollow.

Putting her purse on her shoulder, Korine clutched the envelope containing Judge Pierce's last will and testament. Walking slowly down the stairs, she paused at the landing. The massive oak doors leading into the courtroom on the first floor were open. Judge Pierce had presided there for many years. She had to wonder if he hadn't meted out justice in his own way after he died. She continued on down the stairs and entered the courtroom.

Seating herself on the back row of the gallery, she opened the envelope and unfolded the copy. A brash scrawl met her eyes. She wondered why a judge had resorted to a holographic will. The handwriting was ornate but eminently readable.

"I, Judge Randall K. Pierce, being of sound mind and body do . . ." It went on in the usual fashion. Korine scanned down until she came to the part about The Pines.

"I do so leave this house, an important part of the history of the Pierce family, to the children of my body . . ."

Korine folded her reading glasses and tucked them back in her purse. *Pompous old fool,* she thought. Did he have any idea what he would drive his daughter to do by wording his will this way? She didn't have to read any further to know what had been on Sally Tucker's birth certificate. Or to know who had broken into the courthouse over the weekend. She raised her face to the balanced scales of justice on the wall behind the bench. The lines blurred as tears filled her eyes.

"Aunt Korine, don't cry. You're in plenty of time."

Korine looked up to see Dennis and Katie Anne beaming before her. "What?" she asked.

"You got our message?" Katie Anne asked.

"No," she answered.

Shyly, Katie Anne took Dennis's arm and said, "We're going to have Judge Carrolton marry us. We wanted you to be here."

Korine stood up and hugged both of them. "I'm so glad." She linked her arm through Dennis's arm and walked up to Judge Carrolton's office with them.

Despite the fact that the beginning of their marriage would be very difficult, what with Dennis spending the first little while or so in jail for moving Greg's body, and despite the fact that Susannah failed to attend, it was a beautiful wedding.

CHAPTER TWENTY

"WE MIGHT AS WELL get this over with," Dennis sighed. At Korine's suggestion, the three of them had retired to his small apartment after the ceremony for a quick toast to the happy couple before Korine headed home to change for Greg's funeral. Reluctantly, Dennis picked up the phone and dialed Susannah's number. "Susannah?"

Her shrill voice squawked through the phone.

Dennis winced and switched the phone to the other ear. "Yes, we did get married . . . Even though you weren't there . . . Katie Anne can't come to the phone right now."

In fact Katie Anne was sitting next to Dennis, crying silently.

"We wanted you to be the first to congratulate us."

From the sounds on the other side of the phone, Dennis might have been talking to an irate chicken instead of his new mother-in-law. He put his arm around Katie Anne and dropped a kiss on her forehead. Her tears cleared and she sat up straighter.

Dennis rolled his eyes at Korine. "I know that everyone counted on a big fancy wedding, Susannah. We did too. But our wedding has been taking a backseat to everything going on here in town. We couldn't wait any longer. Once we made up our minds, we just went on down to the courthouse and did it."

Susannah's reply was soft enough that Korine couldn't hear the response from where she sat.

"Thank you. We truly do appreciate the effort you put out for us." Dennis reached out and took Katie Anne's hand. Nodding, his eyes crinkled at the corners as he winked at his new wife. "We're inviting people over to the Green Whistle tonight for dinner. It's not as fancy as the reception we had planned, but Juanita June said that she could do us up a cake." A pause. "I know you do."

Dennis's forehead scrunched up in a frown. Katie Anne traced the wrinkles with a finger and they vanished. Korine again felt that familiar tug of pain in her middle, but this time there was an equal feeling of happiness that helped her keep her balance. These kids wanted her as a part of their family. Charlie was gone, but she still belonged to someone.

"Okay. See you tonight, around six." He placed the receiver gently in the cradle.

Korine looked at her nephew. "That was artfully done. Have you ever considered politics?"

"Not on your life." Dennis shuddered. "She didn't find the message in time," he said, turning to Katie Anne.

"I told her this morning over breakfast. She didn't even look up from her toast."

Dennis and Korine exchanged a look. Both were thinking the same thing: Susannah was not a nice woman.

Korine put her cup by the sink and collected her purse. "I've got to get home and change into something appropriately dark."

"Are you riding with Amilou?"

"No." The abruptness of her reply caught all three of them off guard. "She's riding with her cousins," Korine said, trying to forestall any questions.

"J. J. hasn't said anything else about what evidence he found implicating her?"

"I haven't talked to him."

"But I thought you were her alibi for Sally's murder?"

"Hmm," Korine opened her purse to pull her keys out. "Congratulations." She hugged first Katie Anne, then Dennis. "Many, many happy years together. I'll see you at two, at the funeral home."

As the door to the apartment closed behind her, she heard Katie Anne ask Dennis, "Now what do you suppose that was all about?"

Korine was still undecided what to do about what she had

discovered. Before this week, she would have sworn she knew Amilou inside and out, but events had proven otherwise. She knew that Amilou had been at the courthouse Saturday night, but that didn't mean that she couldn't have killed Sally too. More than ever, she wanted to avoid talking to J. J. But if— despite knowing that Amilou had both motive and opportunity to kill Sally—she hadn't done it, not going to the funeral of her best friend's husband would be unforgivable.

The weight of the Cutlass's door made a satisfying slam as she got into the car. In addition to her worry about Amilou's probable guilt, when she got home she would have to deal with Chaz's questions. He'd almost driven her to distraction asking her opinion on Amilou's newest admissions to him. Korine stepped too hard on the gas as she pulled away from the curb. Her wheels shrieked against the pavement, winding her already too-tight nerves even tighter.

She was halfway home when she looked in her rearview mirror and saw the flash of police lights behind her. Korine pulled into the busy Wal-Mart parking lot. Her heart sank when she saw a grinning J. J. emerge from his car.

"Avoiding me?"

"Of course not," she lied. "You wearing that to Greg's funeral?"

"I was on my way home to change and pick up Janey when I saw you. Couldn't resist flagging you down to get you to officially corroborate Amilou's alibi for Sally's death. You spent Saturday night with Amilou didn't you?"

"Yes."

"Did she leave the house at all?"

Korine tried to speak but couldn't get the words to leave her mouth.

"Oh, hell, Korine. Please don't tell me that Amilou was out in the middle of the night."

"Okay." That word came out of Korine's throat just fine.

"So she *wasn't* home all night?'

"J. J., not now."

He turned and leaned against the scuffed side of Korine's car. "Frieda said that you'd been chasing her all weekend and finally caught up to her this morning."

"You knew?"

"Yep. Had to talk to Judge Carrolton, didn't I, to get search warrants? She called Kathleen Hennessey for me and that's all she wrote."

"What am I going to do, J. J.? I keep thinking that this is Amilou we're talking about. We finish each other's sentences, for goodness' sake. Wouldn't I know if she had done something like this?"

"Welcome to my side of the line, Korine."

"It's not a line, it's a gorge," Korine replied. If J. J. had to look at people that he knew like this every day in the course of his job, then Korine didn't know how he'd stayed with it this long.

He straightened and pulled his hat back down over his forehead. "I won't ask you any more right now. We'll talk after the funeral." He reached out and patted Korine's arm, then walked over to his cruiser and got in.

She wiped her eyes with the back of her hand and keyed the ignition. Following J. J. out onto the road, she turned toward home. Facing Chaz would be a piece of cake compared to this.

CHAPTER TWENTY-ONE

AMILOU LOOKED LIKE DEATH sitting in the front row of the funeral home chapel. Chaz had been his usual efficient self, arranging bail in time for her to attend Greg's funeral. Even though he was here in an official capacity, J. J. pitied her. He would have gone and sat with her, but considering what he was about to do, that would not be a good idea.

Strains of some popular song about loss and grieving filtered down from the speakers hidden in the ceiling. The song wasn't exactly appropriate, because J. J. sure as shooting didn't think Greg was looking down on Amilou from heaven. Much more likely that he was looking up to her now, even though he hadn't done so in life.

As they came in, J. J. had tried to warn Janey about what might happen here. She had stared at him, an unsettlingly knowing expression on her face. Finally, she'd said that she didn't want or need to know what he had in mind to ruin what would already be a horribly memorable occasion. Turning on her heel, she'd gone up front to sit with Amilou, who had come in, alone, to her husband's funeral. Evidently the cousins who were supposed to accompany her to the funeral had cancelled at the last minute.

Amilou had remained essentially alone, as one by one, people came over to her, made a brief comment, then fled from her side. Janey must have looked like a life raft to her, the way she was holding onto Janey's hand.

Chaz came through the door beside J. J., followed by his mother. J. J. reached out and tapped him on the shoulder.

Chaz motioned for Korine to go on ahead as he turned to face J. J.

"Let's step out for a minute," J. J. requested.

"I think Mrs. Klein's second family room is open."

"Good idea. I've got a few things to catch you up on, and it would be nice if we could do it without an audience."

Twenty minutes later, Chaz and J. J. slipped back in. Chaz went on down to join Amilou and Janey. J. J. pulled a folding chair out of the alcove at the back of the room and sat behind the back row. Scanning the audience, he frowned. One of the heads he had expected to see sitting on the front row was gone. Korine was nowhere to be seen.

Chaz's and Amilou's heads were bowed together, Chaz no doubt passing on some of what J. J. had told him. Amilou threw J. J. a dagger of a glance before turning back to gesture vehemently to Chaz. With an effort, J. J. kept his face impassive, although he felt like he'd swallowed a gaggle of geese. Continuing to look around while trying to ignore his restive stomach, he spotted Dennis and Katie Anne sitting on the opposite side of the room from Susannah.

Frowning, J. J. wondered about that seating arrangement. Jancy had given him the good news about the kids' elopement. Although J. J. approved, the covert looks from certain members of the audience, followed by whispers under cover of shielding hands, showed that there were a few people who disagreed with him on this one.

Susannah never once looked in their direction. She must have decided she didn't want someone who'd bury a dead body in her yard as a son-in-law. Given their history, it was predictable that Susannah sat still, staring a hole in the back of Amilou's head, two points of color highlighting her cheeks. J. J. had to wonder if she knew what he was about to do.

He thought it would be helpful if Korine could be present for this. She was still nowhere to be seen. J. J. leaned forward and tapped Hank Jenkins on the shoulder. "Where's Korine?" he whispered.

"She up and—"

"She stormed out of here like a whipped dog. Fighting like that with Amilou on the front row of the funeral parlor!" If Sarah Jane's eyes hadn't shone so brightly, her delivery would have been perfect in its dismay. As it was, J. J. didn't know how Hank had prevented her from getting up to find one of her cronies to help her dissect this tidbit.

"Sarah Jane!" Hank's voice was no less rigid for being delivered in a calm tone of voice. She pressed her lips together and folded her hands in her lap. Only the tap-tap-tap of her toe showed the effort involved in keeping her mouth firmly shut.

Hank gave Sarah Jane one more quelling glance then leaned over the back of the pew to fill J. J. in on Korine's departure. "They had words. No," he said in response to J. J.'s raised eyebrows, "we couldn't hear any of it. But if you ask me, Korine knows something and couldn't stomach it any-more." In contrast to his wife, Hank didn't seem to welcome this news.

"So Korine has made sure everyone in town thinks Amilou's guilty?"

"Seems that way." Hank raised his eyebrows.

J. J. shook his head at Hank. "I'm still not telling. But you'll know soon enough."

Sarah Jane's breath whistled as she gasped. She opened her mouth to ask J. J. a question—or five. Hank firmly grasped her hand and she subsided. J. J. settled back into the cold metal chair and waited for the music to begin.

Reverend Richardson arrived and spent a moment holding Amilou's hand. Whatever he said brought an onset of fresh tears. In contrast, Susannah's cheek spots brightened further. Katie Anne buried her head in Dennis's shoulder, finally giving up on getting her mother's attention. J. J. watched, sat, and waited.

Taking his place at the podium in front of the room, Reverend Richardson began the service. After the usual psalms and platitudes about untimely death, he turned his attention to Amilou. "You have been through a great deal in the last few months. Having talked with you, I understand some of the feelings that you've encountered."

He paused, delivering stern glances to a select few in the crowd before continuing. "Not everyone has been as under-standing of your circumstances as they should have been."

The slender neck in front of J. J. flushed a dull pink. Sarah Jane shifted in her seat and subsided when Hank put his arm around her. Several others in the audience had the same reaction. Interestingly enough, not all of them were the ones that the minister had singled out.

"Losing a husband not once, but twice, has served you poorly. While we cannot know what caused some of Greg's actions, we can only trust that he now understands full-well the consequences of those actions."

Amilou stared unblinking and pale at the Reverend's unusual approach to the traditional funereal summing up of the deceased's attributes. The rest of the audience were similarly stunned.

"Despite the break in your relationship, you continued to care deeply for this man. That is not something for which you need apologize. Love is unusual in its ability to last, despite trying circumstances."

The minister turned his attention to the crowd in general. "We have all had times in our lives that were dark. We do not know who among us is guilty of Greg Whittier's death. Despite the damage that he played out among us, whoever did this played God with Greg's life. You do not have that right. Amilou had the right to feel anger for what Greg did to her, yet she still loved him. There are others among us who were similarly abandoned by Greg, yet they chose to go on with their lives, rather than grasping their pain to their hearts and letting it rot them from the inside out."

Claudia flushed deep red, as did half-a-dozen other young women scattered about the room. J. J. watched closely, but the woman he had his eye on didn't blink an eye.

"Amilou has asked to say a few words about Greg." The Reverend stepped out from behind the podium and Amilou stood up. Walking haltingly, she made her way up the short run of steps to stand next to the closed coffin.

Laying her hand on the polished beech lid, she began. "Thank you for being here. I feel very odd standing before you today eulogizing my almost-ex-husband."

A few twitters broke out. Amilou smiled weakly back.

"I knew Greg Whittier much better than anyone did. Greg was a charmer. He had a way of making me feel that I was the only one he had eyes for. The most beautiful woman in the world. I would have done anything to keep him."

A few gasps from the audience brought a wry smile to Amilou's face. "No, this is not a confession. Although I couldn't help but know about some of the other women he saw from time to time, he married *me*. That meant something." Amilou's eyes hardened as she locked her concentration onto Susannah. "Actually, it meant everything. Because Greg also needed something that only I could give him."

"Money." Susannah stood up. "The only thing you gave him that he couldn't get elsewhere was money."

"Actually, he told me that what I gave him was a feeling of home. No matter what he'd done, I still loved him and let him in at the end of the day. And God help me, If I'd let him in that final day of his life, he'd still be alive."

Susannah had pushed her way out of her row and was stalking down the isle. Wearing the ivory tea-length dress that J. J. had heard so much about from Sarah Jane, she advanced on Amilou and said, "That's ridiculous. He didn't want to go back to you. He had already come home to me."

"Sally told me what she saw after I closed the door on Greg."

Susannah stopped, rocked on her stiletto heals by Amilou's plain words.

"You never talked to Sally, you hated her."

"For a long time, I did blame her, yes." Amilou swallowed. "But I've done a lot of thinking over the past few days. Spending all that time holed up in The Pines has opened my eyes. Greg was not the only one who used people. Sally was just as much a victim as I was. And I'm ashamed to say that I treated her unfairly."

"She deserved it. All she wanted was your money, and when she couldn't get it out of you, she tried to get it through Greg. And she lured him away from you with something you could never give him: a child."

Sarah Jane's gasp from the row in front of him distracted J. J. for a minute. If Hank had looked at all concerned, J. J.

would have thought that Sarah Jane was having a heart attack the way her chest was rising and falling in quick-time. J. J. quickly returned his attention to the two women standing face-to-face on the podium in front of the closed coffin.

Susannah added, "Then she, too, played him false. Sally Tucker aborted their baby."

Amilou's response was drowned out by the collective gasp of the audience. She looked around at the rapt faces of the people who had called themselves friends, and shuddered.

Susannah put her hands on Amilou's shoulders and began to shake her. "Greg only wanted a family. He almost had one once, but you turned him away from us."

Susannah turned her head to Amilou and threw her next words at her like sharp gray stones. "Last Wednesday he rose above that influence. He knocked on my door and came home. Today was to have been our wedding day."

At this, a laugh escaped Amilou. "You can't be serious. Greg came home Thursday night. He begged me to take him back."

"He wouldn't have." Susannah spat the words into Amilou's face.

J. J. hauled himself up out of his chair and started toward the front of the room. Time to shut this catfight down before one of these two women got hurt.

"Why not, Susannah, had you stabbed him already?" Amilou hissed.

"So you admit he never wanted to go back to you?" Susannah shot back.

Chaz looked over at J. J. Nodding in the affirmative, J. J. stopped where he was. Chaz got up and went to stand by Amilou just as Susannah lunged at her.

"What did you promise him if he came back to you?" Susannah asked. "I had his child. What more could you offer him that I couldn't?"

Amilou staggered back, stepping on Chaz. They fell, tangled, into the seat behind them. The whole room rose to keep the two struggling women in their sight. In the midst of the gawking crowd, J. J. saw Katie Anne turn her face into Dennis's shoulder.

Susannah flung her hand up over her head, bringing J. J.'s attention back to her. Down it flashed, fist beating again and again on Amilou's face, arms, and shoulders. The room was in a turmoil of sound, but all J. J. could hear were the words that were coming out of Susannah's mouth.

"It's your fault!" she shouted over and over, punctuating each cry with a blow to Amilou's arms, flung over her head for protection. J. J. grabbed Susannah and hauled her off.

"You made me do it. If you had just given Sally the money, then she wouldn't have stolen Greg away." Susannah's venomous whisper carried throughout the room. "Sally was a selfish, greedy little soul. Like mother, like daughter. Greg, I regret. Her, I enjoyed."

J. J. couldn't believe his luck that Susannah had just confessed in front of a whole town full of witnesses. "I think we've got sufficient witnesses to put her away, what do you think?" he asked.

Chaz held Amilou down as she struggled to rise. Wise move. By the look on her face, she would have started in on Susannah, then J. J. would have had to haul them both off to jail.

Leon bounded forward, pulling his handcuffs—and several other items—out of his pocket as he came. Susannah, predictably enough, struggled violently when he tried to clasp them around her wrists.

"None of that, Susannah. I think we've got enough charges to bring you up on," J. J. said, helping Leon hold her still.

Claudia, two rows back, may have dressed in black for Greg, but her eyes shone for the young officer. Amilou stood, gripping Chaz's hands for dear life, her brown eyes huge in a pale face. Janey pushed her way through the standing crowd and put her arms around Amilou.

"I told you," Janey said smugly.

"You knew?"

"Not all of it," J. J. answered. "Unless she's been listening in on my phone calls."

Janey wrinkled her nose at him.

"All right, people." J. J. raised his hands to try and quiet the crowd as Leon and Jett escorted a still-furious Susannah out to the car. "Suppose we finish up this funeral and let the widow go home."

Amilou looked at him, openly astonished. "J. J. Bascom, Do you really think we can go right back to eulogizing Greg after that?"

"Why not?" Chaz asked.

J. J. sat down next to Janey and waited expectantly. Amilou looked from him to Reverend Richardson to the audience. What she saw there must have made a difference in how she felt, because she took a deep breath and began again.

"I can't top what we've just been through. Can we skip to the closing hymn and go home? I need a drink before I can tell any more Greg stories."

Many in the room smiled at one another as if they had known all along who had really been the murderer. Amilou took her seat of pride in the front row, and the minister took his place behind the podium once again. He led them in a hymn of thanksgiving that J. J. sang with heartfelt feeling.

Afterward, Amilou had her hands full. Everyone in the room felt compelled to come up to her, the effusiveness of their condolences betraying just how many of them really had thought her capable of murder. Forgotten in the melee, Katie Anne and Dennis slipped away.

"That poor child," Sarah Jane said to J. J.

"I think she'll be all right," Amilou said. "After all, she had the good sense to fall in love with Dennis."

"How can you say that?" Sarah Jane's brow puckered in dismay. "He buried Greg in that flower bed!"

Amilou didn't reply to that one, having turned discretely away to discuss something with the Reverend.

Sarah Jane looked after her, then started in on J. J. "Why on earth is she having a private interment? You know that we would all love to be there to support her."

"Amilou decided this yesterday. After all she's been through, she ought to be able to say good-bye to Greg in her own way."

Hank prevented Sarah Jane from arguing her point by

expediently taking her arm and leading her out the door. J. J. put out his hand to Amilou. "Still friends?" he asked.

"I suppose," she answered, taking his hand. "But don't you want to know about Sally?"

"I saw the birth certificate."

Amilou paled.

"Kathleen made a copy after Sally was in looking for it, as well as a copy of your father's will. She got it over to me as soon as we found Sally's body."

"So why didn't you arrest me?"

"A little bird told me you didn't do it." J. J. put his arm around Janey and hugged her. "Now, didn't I just hear Mrs. Hawkins say something about bringing another funeral casserole over to your place? How about we go over and hold down the fort until you're ready to come back home?"

As the small group walked out to the car, J. J. found himself matching steps with Chaz. "Well, counselor, you're short on clients right now. Susannah's going to need a good lawyer. You want a client who's as good as confessed?"

Chaz shuddered delicately. "Thank you, but I believe I need to have a tooth or two pulled this week. Won't be able to talk due to the pain, you see."

"Hope you and I don't wind up on opposite sides of the fence too often. You enjoy yourself far too much doing this."

"Yes." Chaz sounded surprised. "I suppose I do."

"Will you do me a favor?" J. J. turned serious.

"Sure." Chaz hesitated only a fraction of a second.

"Find your mother and make sure she knows what happened in there. Amilou just publicly lost her family reputation in there. She's going to need her friends."

Chaz shook J. J.'s hand. "Gladly. Now all I have to do is find her."

"Try the cemetery." Janey slipped her arm through J. J.'s.

"I appreciate what you're trying to do," Amilou said from behind Chaz. "Ultimately, it's between the two of us, but I sure could use your support. Will you come with me?"

Chaz drew Amilou's trembling arm through his to escort her to the waiting car. "Let's go."

CHAPTER TWENTY-TWO

KORINE SAT BY CHARLIE'S GRAVE. It was her favorite quiet place to go when things troubled her. If ever she needed the solace, this was the time. She had seen the hearse pull in the gate and watched it wind its way around to the plot down the hill from where she sat on a hard concrete bench. Amilou climbed out, followed by Reverend Richardson. The only sounds were those of the fountain on the opposite side of the path and the whip of the wind in the awning covering Greg's open grave. Amilou looked up once but gave no sign that she had seen Korine.

Korine couldn't hide from herself any longer that she had come to Charlie's grave to escape the fact that she had failed her friend. She hadn't even found out how Amilou had gotten out of jail before flying at her. Amilou's insistence that she hated Sally had undone all of Korine's good intentions, allowing her fear and anger to dictate her actions rather than reason and sense.

Chaz pulled his Suburban in behind the hearse and climbed out. Shading his eyes with one hand, he looked up at Korine. When he started toward her, she found that it took a conscious effort to still the trembling of her hands. She waited, cold as the bench she rested upon, to see what he would do.

He took his time coming up the hill. Behind his climbing form, Korine could see the men from the funeral home shoulder their burden. The sleek, light-colored coffin glinted in the sunlight. Korine blinked and put one hand up to block the reflected daggers of light.

"Mother." Chaz's tone was cool as he greeted her.

Not trusting herself to speak, Korine slid over so that he

could join her.

"Let's go walk a bit, shall we?" Chaz asked. Putting out his hand, he freed one of Korine's ice-cold hands from the other and gave it a tug. "J. J.'s got his woman, Mom, and it's not your friend."

"Thank goodness." Korine's voice cracked as she stood up beside her son. Unreasonably, she tried to explain herself to him. "But she broke into Sally's and trashed her place, and she was out at all the wrong times. Her knife was even gone, Chaz. Everything fit."

"She's guilty of some things, but not murder. The knife was in the potting shed, used to divide bulbs a few weeks ago. She'll have to pay a price for breaking and entering at Sally's. But not murder. Susannah confessed."

Korine stumbled, the heel of her shoe sinking deep into the shorn grass. "Confessed?" Her voice was breathless.

"In front of God and everybody." There was a world of satisfaction on Chaz's face. It faded as he looked down at his mother's upturned face. "You left too soon."

Korine felt her joy pierced by the shame of having deserted her friend. She turned her face away from the uncompromising stare her son gave her. She watched, instead, as the men carrying Greg's coffin placed it on the metal supports and walked a few paces away. One of them tugged at his collar as Amilou selected a stem from one of the many sprays of flowers lining the graveside.

"I know," Korine said softly. "I knew before you came up here and told me about Susannah." She let go of Chaz's arm and knelt by Charlie's grave. One hand rested on the headstone. "What should I do?" she asked, afraid of the answer.

"Open your eyes." Chaz put out his hand and pulled her back up once again. "Look down there. That woman is the best friend you've ever had. She still needs you. Are you going to let her down again?" Abruptly, Chaz let go of her and started back down the hill. When he got to the bottom, he went over to Amilou and gave her a hug, then turned and went to his car.

Korine caught her breath. The flower that Amilou held was

a bright pink amaryllis from Korine's offering. She stood for a minute by the coffin. Raising her face once, she wiped at it with her hand. The minister hugged her, then walked away, not without several backward glances. When he studiously looked up the hill toward Korine and shielded his eyes with one hand, she understood what Amilou was doing.

Korine hesitated, looking down toward her friend. Amilou stood, just as uncertainly, at the other end of the long path between them.

The warmth of the sun beat down upon Korine's shoulder blades, feeling almost like the comfort she used to draw simply from the gentle touch of Charlie's hand on the small of her back. It was as if Charlie were exhorting her not to waste any more time. She stepped out down the hill toward Amilou. When she reached the bottom, the two women stood, face-to-face.

Korine reached out and encircled her friend, being careful not to crush the stem that Amilou still held in her hand. "I am so sorry that I doubted you."

"And I'm sorry that I lied to you. I was so afraid." Amilou's face was wet with tears.

"I was too," Korine said, knowing that her own face was as damp and shiny as Amilou's.

"J. J. says that I'm still in a heap of trouble over the breaking and entering, but he thinks that the judge will give me community service."

Korine took a deep breath and asked, "Can we still be friends?"

"We have to be." Amilou's brown eyes looked steadily at Korine.

Reverend Richardson came up and put his arm around Amilou's shoulders. "Shall we begin the ceremony now that everyone you wanted present is here?" Amilou smiled at Korine, a simple uncomplicated smile. Korine felt her lips twitch in response.

Amilou walked forward and placed her hand on the lid of the coffin. "You know," she said, a catch in her voice. "I truly loved Greg when I married him. And with a few notable exceptions, he was a good husband to me. But you know what? He never found happiness. That's not the epitaph I want on my gravestone. It's time to move on."

She paused and looked at her hand resting on the smooth lid of Greg's coffin. Amilou moved it a little, as if caressing the wood. "Good-bye," she whispered.

Reverend Richardson began his final prayer. Once done, Amilou stooped. Korine remembered how the grit of the obligatory final handful of dirt had felt as it filled her palm. Breathing in, she took in the smells of freshly turned dirt, blooming vines, and wilting flowers. She found her own fingers curling in sympathy for Amilou.

Opening her hand, Amilou let the dirt go. It fell with the softness of rain, making barely a sound as it landed. Turning away, she walked a few paces away from the grave as the men moved in to finish up.

"I see why you like to visit Charlie," Amilou said. "It's calm here."

Korine nodded and tucked Amilou's cold hand through the crook of her arm. "Let's walk up and let him know we're going to be all right," she suggested.

Korine had found that like her own garden early in the morning, there was a calm here that could be captured and held. She had never shared it with anyone before. It was much better with company than alone. Amilou was right. It was time to move on.

Leaving the men finishing the job of covering Greg's final resting place, Amilou and Korine walked up the hill. Their voices were silent, their footsteps steady. They were content to allow their friendship to heal in its own time.